WHAT FOOLS WE HAVE BEEN

HANK WILLIAMS

Chiselbury

Cover by Jamie Keegan

Published by Chiselbury Publishing, a division of Woodstock Leasor Limited
14 Devonia Road, London N1 8JH, United Kingdom

www.chiselbury.com

ISBN: 978-1-917837-45-3 (hardback)

ISBN: 978-1-917837-35-4 (paperback)

ISBN: 978-1-917837-36-1 (ebook)

A CIP catalogue record for this book is available from the British Library

CONTENTS

PART I
THE WALK

Jess 3
Simon 17
David 28
Ruth 36

PART II
AN IMAGINED LIFE

The Ball 51
The Shop 60
The House 71
The Funeral 83

PART III
END OF LIFE CARE

Morris 95
Charlie 104
David 113

PART IV
INHERITANCE

Irene 127

Acknowledgments 141
Also by Hank Williams 143

For my mother

PART I

THE WALK

JESS

JESS IS FURIOUS! When her mum told her, she screamed!

She felt like she was being evacuated, like she was being banished.

She had plans, plans for the summer. It's like her plans count for *nothing*! She is *fourteen years old*!

She tried everything to persuade her mum. She failed. Kate was insistent: "you're coming."

In the car, on the way up, Jess refused to be there. She was *not* in the car.

Tom walled off behind his earphones, playing his stupid

games, but what she is doing is different, this is refusing to be in the car when you are in the car.

She is on her phone to her friends, they are outraged: 'she can't do that!', 'you've been kidnapped!', 'it's abuse!'. She takes heart from their outrage.

What is her dad *doing*?

Why is her mum *doing* this?

She refuses to look out the window. Such a long journey, such a long way, miles from anywhere. Exile. *Why*?

She is on the back seat with Tom. There is no way she will sit in the front, next to her mother. She scrunches down by the door with her phone, trying to ignore Tom's game grunts and twitches.

Kate's new company car. Leg room. Leather seats. The smell of its newness is making her feel sick. She opens the window a little. At least she can charge her phone.

Her mum doesn't try to talk to her. That's something. But not even sorry!

They get held up in traffic somewhere, a place called Stafford, and Kate goes on a rant about smart motorways and Jess sees that she is angry too and realises that nobody wants to be doing this, which helps a bit.

She has been there two times already this year, her grand-dad's house, *twice already!* It is in the middle of nowhere, there is nothing there. *Nothing!*

Jess screams. She didn't mean to. She forgot where she was. Tom hears it even through those earphones. He glares at her:

"What the fuck!"

Kate shouts over her shoulder:

"That's enough!"

When they get to the house, Simon is in the doorway waiting for them. Jess can tell he doesn't want them there. Her mum doesn't want them; her dad doesn't want them. Great! Tom throws himself at his dad and Simon takes hold of him but he is looking at Kate. Because Jess isn't *in* the car, she doesn't get *out* of the car. Kate has to shout: "Jess!" Then she moves.

What does she actually know? She knows her parents are separated, that they are probably going to divorce. *Great!* She knows that her mum is worried about her dad and is also furious with him. She knows her mum has told her dad that the kids must stay with him for at least some of the summer. She knows that her dad shouldn't be here in his parents' house but he is, he is somehow stuck here, he has been here for weeks, and this is driving her mum mad and worrying her. She is trying not to worry the kids, but clearly there is something wrong, which makes them being here even more stupid: *we're not the adults here.*

And to make matters worse, it's her period and she feels like shit.

"Hi Jess," Simon says, not quite looking at her.

Simon doesn't know how to be with Jess, whatever he does will be wrong.

"Hi," she manages.

They haven't seen him for a while, not in person. He looks bad, he has made an effort, he's shaved, and he still looks bad. Thin and grey. Like a weasel. He's been weird since his father died and that's like, *yes*, but it has gone on too long, that's what she overheard Kate saying to him on the phone: 'this has gone on too long.' But hey: *here are the kids, get on with it.*

The house is half empty. He came here to clear the house and it's like he's half-cleared it, there's furniture, but all the little things are gone, and now he is living here, so it's like they will be *camping* here. The three of them are looking at the place: it's too weird, it's like *what the fuck, dad?*

Jess wants to go to her room but she doesn't know which room is hers. When they were here before, when grandad was ill, when he was dying, though she didn't know that at the time *because they didn't tell her*, they had stayed in a house in the village. They stayed there for four long days and they came every day to see him. What do you say? There is nothing to say: after the first day, you sit there and its sad and he is so tired. You look back and you think, if I had known, *if someone had told me*, and then: what? what would she have done differently? How many times can you tell your grandad that you love him? She was glad when they left, and then they came back for the funeral, which was *ok*, she got that, but now here they are again, for the third time, and there is no grandad and it is the last place she wants to be. It's way too weird. It's creeping her out.

Simon lets them into the house.

Tom moves towards the living room and the tv but Kate says:

"Tom! No!"

He looks at her as if there are literally no other options for him. He is twelve years old.

Kate says to Simon: "put the kettle on."

"Of course," he says.

He moves into the kitchen and Kate follows him and Tom follows Kate.

"I need a hot water bottle," says Jess.

"Right," says Simon, looking at Kate helplessly.

He has taken the hot water bottles to the tip.

"I packed one," says Kate. "I'll get it."

Simon puts more water in the kettle.

They have given her Howard's room. *Really*! Her dead uncle Howard. That freaks her out even more. They must have known it would freak her out. She says:

"Tom can have it."

Tom says: "no way!"

Jess shuts her eyes. "*Fine*."

She goes upstairs and throws herself on the bed and thinks:

'Piss off Howard, I don't give a shit,' and then she feels bad and says out loud: "sorry."

She tells her friends. They are outraged, again. They don't believe it. They want to know: is it haunted? *Great*!

Her mum brings up her hot water bottle and Jess takes it and turns her face to the wall. Kate doesn't make her say thank you.

The room smells like it hasn't been a room for a long time: old and musty, sad, empty. A bed, a table, a chair, a chest of drawers, a wardrobe. The walls are bare except for the marks where posters had been. The mattress is ok. The bed creaks. It's like she's in prison.

Kate stays for two nights. The four of them haven't been together for weeks. For a moment, it feels normal, and then it doesn't. There are moments when they forget it isn't normal and it's normal again: the four of them together. The first night, Kate has brought food that she heats up in the microwave and Simon lays the table. Chinese: spring rolls; sweet and sour chicken; egg fried rice; vegetable chow mein. Tom is happy. There is no soy sauce. *Whatever*. To Jess it tastes of nothing, chemicals maybe.

On the second night, Kate and Simon sit them down in the living room and that's enough for them to know.

"You're getting divorced," says Tom, accusingly.

"Yes," says Kate.

"Are you going to be living up here?" Jess asks Simon.

"I think so."

Kate closes her eyes.

"When will we see you?" Tom looks at his dad.

"Whenever you want."

"That's not an answer," says Jess.

"She's right," says Kate.

"You'll see me," says Simon.

"That's not good enough," says Jess.

"You're here now. I'm here. You're seeing me."

Kate sighs: "one step at a time."

"It's so far," says Jess and she starts to cry.

Once Kate has gone, things could go wrong, but they don't. Jess is through her period. Tom wants to please. Simon makes an effort. They love their dad. They are almost sure that he loves them. They *are* sure that he loves them, but right this minute, it might be that he hasn't got the capacity to love them very much. Kate had used that word - capacity, as in: 'your dad hasn't got a lot of capacity right now'. Tom had asked: 'so, *what*? so what does that even *mean*?' Jess had said: 'go gentle' and Kate had said: 'be patient'. '*Right*,' said Tom.

But once Kate has gone, Simon feels better. They had talked, the kids heard them talking, didn't hear what they said, but they were talking and as Jess said to Tom: 'that's better than not talking'. Tom said to her: 'rich coming from you' and she told him to piss off but he had a point. 'Ok,' she said. Kate left in the morning, and they think that, for the rest of the day, they will be left to their own devices, literally, but Simon says 'let's go for a walk.' They are so surprised that they say yes. He tells them he will take them on the walk he used to do with his dad when he was their age. Jess asks: 'how long?' and Tom says: 'Jess!'. Simon smiles: 'not that long'.

They walk through woods and over fields, cross roads and stiles. It's wet, it's muddy, it's slippery, but Jess says nothing and Tom even enjoys it, being outdoors, fresh air, who knew? It's cloudy but it is not raining and it is warm. It's ok. She's not cold, which is what she thought she would be. She likes the big rocks that are scattered loosely on the ground. How did that happen? How did they get there? Tom climbs onto a big block and bets her she can't do it, but she does, second go. They sit on it together. Simon laughs with pleasure and takes a photo of them on his phone, he says he'll send it to Kate, as if it was proof of something. He tells them that it is the same rock that he and his brother used to fight over when they were boys. Tom stands and lets out a roar. They look around: they are surrounded by fields divided by grey stone walls. There is a group of sheep resting in the shade of an oak tree. There are no other people in sight. They are the only human beings in the world right now.

They walk up to a spot which overlooks the Bay. Tom sees what might be a cave in the cliff face to their right and asks if he can explore. He scampers off, back down the hill, and clatters over the stones that mark the shoreline, threaded with debris washed up by the tide. Simon asks Jess if she is ok.

"Are *you* ok?" she says.

A sudden brightness in the sky, ignoring the clouds, electrifies the Bay with flashes of silver. Simon points at a heron, bathed in the light, standing close by on the sand, neck coiled, so, so still.

"Is it alive?" whispers Jess, "what is it doing?"

"Waiting."

"What for?"

"I don't know."

'Like you, dad,' thinks Jess.

Just then, the heron hauls itself off the ground, such an effort, and flaps low and languorously in search of some privacy. It seems to be flying sideways.

"Is it stoned?" asks Jess.

Simon chuckles.

"Can you smell the sea?" he asks her.

She breathes in; she realises that she can, a distant salt tang.

"Yes," she says, closing her eyes.

Tom returns.

"Was anybody inside?" Simon asks him.

"You can go inside," says Tom, "it's not big, but you could camp there."

Simon tells them that their grandad, David, came here, to this spot, every day for forty days before he got too ill, and he took a photograph of exactly the same view.

"Why?"

"Every day was different."

"Really?"

"Yes. The weather would be different. The light, the tide. And every day he made a note of what he was thinking about. I found a folder on his laptop, forty-one days. I turned it into a book. I'll show you when we get home."

That evening, after he has cooked them some pasta with sauce from a jar and Tom has cleared away and Jess has washed up without arguing, he shows them the book. In amongst the photographs of the Bay, which seem all the same to them, there are photographs of people, and they find those more interesting, Jess in particular.

"Who is she?" Jess asks, pointing at a picture of a handsome woman with bouffant hair.

"That's your grandad's mother, Ruth. She's your great grandmother."

Jess looks at him. "You've never talked about her."

Simon shakes his head.

"Who's that?" asks Tom, pointing at a picture of a woman kneeling in a garden.

"That's my mother, Hannah. Your grandma."

Hannah had died four years before Tom was born.

"She's lovely," says Jess. A thick forest of curly brown hair.

"She was," says Simon. He turns the pages.

"Those are of your brother Howard?" asks Jess, looking at four pictures of a boy, different ages, laid out in a grid.

"Yes, they are."

"Wow," says Tom, "he looks cool."

"Yes. He was," says Simon.

On the last page, there is a photograph of a young woman, a few years older than Jess.

"Who is that?" asks Jess.

"That is my aunt," says Simon. "She is called Irene. Your grandad's sister."

"I didn't know you had an aunt," says Jess.

"I've never met her," says Simon.

"Wow," says Tom. "How come?"

"I don't know," says Simon, shaking his head. "I don't know."

"Why is there no picture of you?" Tom asks.

"There isn't, that's all," says Simon, and he closes the book.

Jess asks if she can take the book up to bed with her. She sits at the table in Howard's empty room. She turns to the black and white photograph of her great grandmother, Ruth, who is looking straight back at her. The top of her dress looks very 60's, hoops of colour, Jess imagines oranges and browns. No earrings. She is beautiful. She takes a pic of the photo and sends it to her friends, saying 'this is my great grandmother.' Lots of likes.

Jess is drawn to the photograph of Irene at the back of the book. She is her dad's aunt. Irene is not pretty but she is attractive: her hair is blowing in the wind, she is smiling, she has good teeth. She seems so sure of herself, she seems so sure of her future. Was she? What happened to her? Why has nobody ever mentioned her? Is she still alive? She looks again at the picture. She envies Irene her self-confidence. She wonders: is there anything of her in me? She sends a pic to her friends, saying 'my mysterious great aunt.'

Jess turns back to the four pictures of Howard. Here she is in his room, what was his room, there is little sign of him now, you would never know. She has heard her father talk about Howard, she knows that he committed suicide, it is very sad. She looks at the four photographs; she wants to say something.

"Hi," she says. "Hi Howard."

The photographs look back at her.

"Do you mind me being here?" Jess asks him. "In your room?"

He looked so happy as a little boy, a big beaming smile.

"What happened? What happened to you?"

The second photograph, maybe she is imagining it, she thinks she can see signs, even then, he is not beaming, he is smiling but there's something not right.

"I wish you could talk to me," she says.

The third photograph, Howard in a school uniform and she can almost see him trying to shake it off, like a skin.

Jess wants to tell him about her, about how bad she feels sometimes, how she doesn't fit anywhere, how she is miserable. She wants to tell him how she feels now, here, in his room, in this house, with her dad, her mum miles away and them not together and the future so bleak, so uncertain. She wants him to say something, her uncle, to comfort her, and then she looks at the photo of Howard as a teenager, how he so clearly doesn't want to be there, framed in that photo, trapped by it.

"Oh Howard," she sounds hoarse. "I'm so sorry."

She puts the book down. She thinks about the people in the book: Ruth. Hannah. Howard. Irene. She thinks about how little she knows about them, how little she has been told, how little she has asked. She wonders what they might think of her. She sees herself as so much her own person - what if she's wrong? She must carry pieces of all of them inside of her, like a mosaic. Maybe she is just the latest version. Maybe she's not who she thinks she is at all.

The next day, she announces to Simon:

"I want to do a family tree."

He looks at her.

"Okay," he says, hesitantly. "Okay."

"Will you help me?"

"Of course."

He sets her up in his father's old office, a big sheet of paper on the desk, pencils, ruler, different coloured pens, highlighters. He is going to leave her to it.

"Wait," she says, "I need you."

"I'll just go and check on Tom."

"He'll be fine."

Tom is fine, and Simon comes back.

"What do you need from me?" he asks.

They start to plot the names on the chart: Jess and Tom at the bottom, with Kate and Simon, their parents, above them, joined by an equal sign, though Jess thinks: *if they are getting divorced?*

"So: your parents are David and Hannah?" she asks her dad.

"Yes," says Simon.

Jess writes these in.

"And you have a brother, Howard?"

"Had a brother."

"Ok. How old was when he died?"

"He was coming up to his twenty-first birthday. Do you want dates?"

"No," says Jess, "I don't think so. I want to know what people were like."

"You want traits?"

"Yes."

"Ok," says Simon, smiling. "Traits not dates."

"Let's get the names down first," says Jess.

"Ok. David's parents were Ruth and Charlie. My grandparents."

Simon points to where they should go.

"I have never heard of Charlie." Jess looks at her father.

"Well."

"There is no photograph of him in the book."

"No," says Simon.

"Why not?"

"Never mind."

Never mind, thinks Jess, *never mind what?*

"Do you know any further back?" she asks her dad, as the rain starts to tap against the window. Simon switches on his father's old angle poise desk light.

"Not much. I know Ruth's mother died young. In the war."

"Woah. What about her dad?"

"He died much later, in 1978, I think. He was called Morris."

"How do you spell that?"

Simon spells it out for her.

Jess writes 'Morris' near the top of her piece of paper.

"What are you doing?" asks Tom, who has wandered in and has been watching them for a while.

"Family tree," says Jess.

"No dates," says Tom critically.

"Traits not dates," Jess and Simon say together and smile at each other.

"What?" says Tom.

"Doesn't matter," says Jess. She doesn't want Tom to be involved.

"Am I Jewish?" asks Tom, "That's a trait, isn't it?"

Jess groans. Tom and his 'am I Jewish' thing.

"You know you're not Jewish," she says crossly.

"It goes down the maternal line," says Simon.

"And mum isn't Jewish?" asks Tom.

"He knows she's not," says Jess.

"What about grandad?" asks Tom.

"Yes. Grandad David was Jewish," says Simon.

"Was grandma Jewish?" asks Tom.

"Yes," says Simon. He had been the one to marry outside.

"So, you're Jewish?" asks Tom.

"Yes," says Simon.

"So, I'm part Jewish?" asks Tom.

"This isn't about being Jewish," says Jess irritably.

"*Okay*," says Tom, sulkily.

"What about Irene?" Jess asks her father, wanting to get back to her tree. "Grandpa's sister."

"What about her?"

"Is she still alive?" she asks.

"I don't know."

"Woah," says Tom, "that's weird. What's that about?"

"It's a long story," says Simon.

Jess writes 'Irene' with a question mark next to David on the family tree, underneath Ruth and Charlie, who are joined by an equal sign. She would like Irene to still be alive. She would like to know her story. She draws a circle around Irene.

"What's that for?" asks Tom.

Simon says: "she is the missing piece."

Jess smiles at her dad. "Well, we've got all summer," she says.

"Yes, we have," says Simon.

"*Oh no!*" groans Tom, but he doesn't mean it.

Jess' family tree

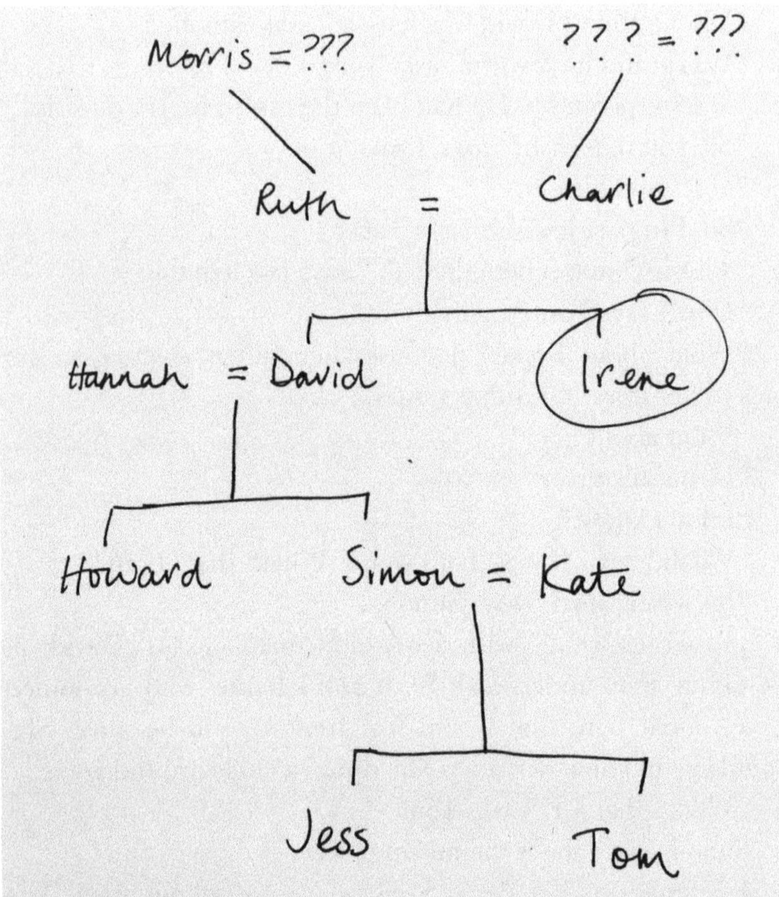

SIMON

THE DAY after David's funeral, Simon went to his father's house with the intention of starting the process of clearing it out. He had hoped that his wife might offer to help him, but she didn't. He had thought that he might ask her, at the funeral, if she would be willing to come with him, but he had failed to do so. Instead, Kate left the crematorium with the children, placing a consoling hand on his arm as she said goodbye. He is alone when he turns the key in the lock and walks through the doorway into the hall. He thought it would take a week to clear, maybe two. The house is near the border between Lancashire and Cumbria. It is a long way from London.

Kate is not yet his ex-wife, but she is no longer his wife. He is waiting for her to ask for a divorce. He hopes that she might change her mind, that she might drift back to him in a reversal of the way that they had drifted apart, that their relationship might be governed by a natural process, that this time the tide had taken her further away from him than before, that is all, but that it will nonetheless bring her back to him, that he is the unmoving shore and she is the restless sea and that they will be reunited again. But he knows this not to be the case.

His father's house, his father's life, the process of clearing out. He stands inside the front door, unable to move. The house without David seems alien, impenetrable. It is his childhood home but still Simon feels that he is trespassing and that soon an alarm will sound, or that someone will appear and ask indignantly what he is doing here. There is an invisible doorway to be gone through, a doorway made up of time and memory, a dense weave that will require determination to breach, a deep breath, a closing and opening of the eyes, a decision.

Kate had loved this house, a converted barn, set apart from the village, so far away from the known world, so different from the town houses she had lived in. Flagstones on the floor, the bare wooden staircase, the paintings on the wall of fells and mountains, the bowls and vases made by Simon's mother, Hannah, the solid wooden doors, the windows. On a clear day, you can see - beyond the fields and their trees and their stone walls - the soft tops of distant hills, their colour changing with the light, from yellow to brown to purple to grey.

Kate had loved her father-in-law, David, too. They would do the crossword together, they would sit and talk, or go for walks, leaving Simon with the children, and he had thought: how is it that he can be like this with you? how is it that you can arrive at this easy affinity, when I ...? After Simon's brother Howard had died, after he had committed suicide. Even before. Ever? Was there ever any attachment between father and son, between David and I? Memories change over time, they warp under the pressure of events, they fade with repetition, they disappear with embarrassment. Kate will not want to come back to this house without David here to greet her.

Simon's father was no hoarder. Going to the tip and coming back with the car empty was one of his pleasures in later life. But even so, there seems to be so much more stuff when there is no one to breathe life into it, things become heavier, they dig their heels in. And then there are the piles of memories: they stack themselves in corners, fold themselves away in drawers and cupboards, attach themselves to objects. Simon is used to the haunting memories of his brother, Howard, and of his mother, Hannah, but now there is the newly minted ghost of his father, David, to add to his confusion. He had escaped this house as soon as he could, travelled south to London, reversing his father's migration northwards, and yet here he is. David's ghost will surely be smiling to itself, amused to see his son back home, alone, as he, David, had been for so many years.

Where to start? Today, Simon thinks, it might be best to sort through the memories for now, put them into boxes, or bin bags, think about what to do with them, whether to keep or to discard. Memories of his brother, for example. David had cleared Howard's room after Hannah had died. Simon had helped him to do it. But now, even in the empty room, memories of Howard hover here, his highs and lows, the sweet periods of calmness, too brief, when contact was possible and hope flickered. The sound of his mother weeping in the hall. David by the front door, waiting for the ambulance, tight and tired, wanting this not to be happening again.

Simon is forty-one years old. He looks older. In the kitchen, he goes to the door that leads to the garden and remembers standing here in shock, his mother sat at the table telling him about her illness, her failing heart, so soon after Howard, less than two years, a world falling apart piece by piece. Kate was with David on the sofa in the sitting room, leaving Simon alone with Hannah, his feelings attacking him, panic, anger, grief. She came to stand next to him, put her arm though his, looked out at the garden, her creation, and at the borrowed landscape of fields and trees, leaned her head against his shoulder. No words. He put his arm around her. They stood there for a while.

"Let me cook tonight," he had suggested.

"Oh, would you?"

Now, in David's office, with the view of the oak trees in the field beyond the garden, and one of his mother's vases in the window, filled with dried hydrangea heads, faded and frail, Simon finds on the desk, to his surprise, a jigsaw. Did his father do jigsaws? He can see, without looking at the box, even though the puzzle is barely half-finished, that it is Constable's Hay Wain. Really? Did David like The Hay Wain? There is the cottage on the banks of a stream, does it still exist, that cottage? Surely it would have been swept away by now by rising waters, or abandoned, who would want to live there, it would be impossible to insure.

Simon picks up a piece of the jigsaw, but after a few attempts to find its rightful place, he returns it to the pile it came from. He wonders if he should feel an obligation to finish the puzzle, for his father's sake; would David want him to? He decides not, and scoops the loose pieces back into the box and then takes a childish pleasure in breaking up the completed sections, turning them back into a collection of fragments, adding them to the others. He puts the lid on firmly to make sure that they don't escape. Charity shop.

He takes David's laptop down from a shelf and opens it. His father had twice taken him through the various folders and files that contained the information he would need to execute the estate. Simon had paid attention the second time, had made notes, had been impressed by the thoroughness, by the care that his father had taken to simplify matters. Kate had told him that he should be more appreciative. He wished he had been now.

There is one folder that he is unfamiliar with. It sits in the middle of the screen. It is called '*Focus!*'. Simon is sure that this folder was not there the last time David had taken him through his files. Has he left it there for him to find, or, like the jigsaw, did he become too ill to finish with it? Should he open it or drag it to the trash? He opens it, thinking that there might be some final instructions inside. There are forty-one files, one for each year of my life thinks Simon fleetingly, but no, he opens the first file, which was created just under five months ago, and it is nothing to do with him, of course not, it is titled Day 1. There is a photograph of a section of Morecambe Bay and underneath the photograph is the date, the 10th of March, and a comment about the view; it is sunny and the tide is out - it has left behind a large island of water surrounded by a sea of sand - and his father writes that he feels heartened by this, grateful to be alive on such a fine spring day.

Simon studies each of the forty-one files in the folder. He marvels that David has been able to take a photograph of exactly the same scene each time – how did he do that? – and he appreciates the subtle differences from day to day, the changes in the weather, the light, the tide, the patterns of the water, the birds. He is fascinated by the emergence of the salt marsh, hard to see clearly until he sets Day 1 beside Day 41. He is moved by his father's writing, which becomes more personal and more thoughtful as the days progress, and then towards the end, shorter, as he becomes weaker.

That first night, Simon sleeps on the sofa in the living room. His old room is now a spare room, full of stuff, and he can't bring himself to sleep in Howard's room, or his parents', not yet. The next morning, he thinks: I must make a start. He decides to go through David's clothes. Almost everything goes into bin bags to be taken to the tip. In the wardrobe there is a suit, he can't remember the last time he saw his father in a suit, and he thinks: charity shop. Kate would know, she would be so much better at this. There is also a coat, a faded brown colour, long, it has a certain glamour. When he lifts it off the rail and tries it on, he is surprised by how heavy it is, the label says camel hair, really? David owned a camel hair coat? Charity shop, he thinks, but then he thinks: Oh Kate, and then: it's too good. I will keep it. For a while.

He takes the bin bags to the tip and when he comes back, he gravitates without thinking to the office and sits down at the desk and opens the laptop and then the folder titled '*Focus!*' and then the file numbered Day 33. It is on this day that David first wrote about life cycles, and what he wrote had touched Simon deeply. Now, as he looks at the photograph, he thinks about his relationship with Kate and how they might have reached the end of its life cycle and how this wasn't necessarily a bad thing, it was perhaps natural and fitting and the problem lay in his struggle to accept it. Kate knew. She hadn't used those words, but this was what she was trying to tell him. He thought: if I can just accept it, would it be easier? How do I accept it? What stops me? The photograph of Day 33 shows a thin strip of sand pushing back at the sea, gulls wheeling overhead, a grey sky turning the water a matching grey; it is what it is, the cycles and the rhythms, the to and fro, this is life. If Kate was here now, he would say to her: 'you are right'. He would like to think that he might say: 'I am grateful for the time we have had together and now I accept that it has come to a natural end'. He would say: 'this is not a failure, not my failure, not yours. Our life cycle has run its course, that is all'.

Simon wonders what David would like him to do with '*Focus!*'. Had he intended anyone to see it? Had he wanted it to be circulated amongst his dwindling group of friends? Had he wanted to publish it in some form? It seems a shame to leave it unseen on David's laptop. He cannot bring himself to drag it to the trash. He persuades himself that in fact David has deliberately left the folder on the desktop because he *did* want his son to find it and to read it and to like it, for it to be part of his estate, and for his executor to do something with it, who knows what? No need to go through probate. Definitely not charity shop.

He looks through the files again. He stops at Day 11. Underneath the photograph, David has written:

'A perfect day, the tide half out, warmth in the sun, the squeals of the oystercatchers. Last night I dreamt about my mother. Such a surprise, and so nice to see her again. I am so glad that I brought her here. I would like her to be standing next to me now.'

Simon does not understand what his father means by this, David's mother died a long time ago, but he says to himself: 'well, I can put her next to you now, Dad'. On a shelf above the desk is a black and white photograph of Ruth. Simon has always liked this picture, has regretted that he never met his grandmother, and he takes the photograph from its frame and scans it on his father's printer. He inserts a new page in the file for Day 11 and drags the scanned photo onto this page and underneath it he types: *Ruth.* There. There she is.

He stops again at Day 22. The tide is fuller now and the sky cloudy. Here David has written:

'A long skein of geese, high above me, chattering. They seem happy together. I am so lonely today.'

It is not that Simon had not felt sorry for his father; he had, how could you not, to lose a son and then your wife so quickly. But, after Hannah's death, David retreated into the dark quarters of himself, he did not make himself available to receive feelings of any kind and Simon was too overridden by his own to be able to work out what might be suitable to offer his father. Now, he feels great sadness for David, feels his loneliness as if it were his own. He regrets that he was not by his father's bedside when he died, that he had not managed to return in time. He goes to the photo library on the laptop and looks for a picture of his mother - a particular photo: Hannah on her knees in the garden, trowel in hand, laughing up at David as he takes the picture - which Simon finds and drags onto the page he has inserted in file 22, and underneath it he types: '*Hannah*'.

On Day 36, the picture shows that the tide is starting to turn. There must be a strong wind because the sea is agitated, wrinkled by small waves. The clouds are low and it is misty. There are no birds. It is bleak. It is as if the bay is being rubbed out, that someone with a rubber is erasing the beauty that is there, taking it away for ever. Is that what causes David to think of Howard this morning? He has written beneath the image: '*my son,*' that is all. My son. Simon is caught by those words. He thinks: who am I then? But more than that he thinks of Howard. He thinks again of life-cycles. Who's to say? Who decides? Did Howard decide? Did he? Did the undertow drag him down? He thinks of Howard before they knew about his condition, so bright, so quick, even then Simon knew that, compared to his brother, he was a lesser being. He opens the photo library again and looks for pictures of Howard. He finds four: baby, toddler, schoolboy, teen; these pictures don't show all of who Howard was; they show the best of him. He inserts a page and drags the four photos onto the blank space, arranges them in two rows of two and under each photo he types: '*my son*'. At the bottom of the page, he types: '*life cycle*'.

The last file, Day 41. Simon looks at the picture of the Bay that David took that day. There is a wide stretch of sand now before you reach the water and if you look closely, you can see that there is a figure there and that their arm is raised. It is the first time a human being has been in one of the photographs. Underneath the image, David has written: '*my sister*'. Simon immediately thinks: she can't be. His father never spoke about his sister. It is as if she didn't exist. This figure on the sand must have reminded David of Irene, how strange after all these years. Simon can see that she is a young woman, her hair blowing in the wind. It looks like she might be waving, perhaps she called out to him.

Underneath '*my sister*', David has added: '*what fools we have been*'. Who does he mean? Simon asks himself. Is he talking about himself, his sister, the two of them? It is his final comment, is he anticipating that someone will find his folder, is he including them in that *we*, is he assuming it will be me? Is he saying to me that *we*, he and I, have been fools for the way we have missed each other. Doubtful. But so much time lost. So much avoidable suffering. Perhaps David is referring to humankind and, as he prepares to die, he is commenting on its talent for destruction. Simon thinks about himself. He thinks: what a fool *I* have been. Can we ever stop ourselves from being the fools we were born to be?

On a shelf in the wardrobe in his parents' bedroom, Simon had found some old photographs in a shoebox. He had taken them to the office and put them on the desk, thinking he might look at them later. He sifts through them now, and finds a picture of a young woman, maybe fifteen years old, smiling, hair blowing. She reminds him of Howard, her eyes, her smile. On the back of the photograph there is a name - Irene - nothing else. Well. There she is. He scans the photograph, inserts a page in the file and pastes the image there. Underneath he types: '*Irene.*'

Simon wonders what he should do now. He thinks at first that he should just delete the folder, with its forty-one files. Then he thinks that he would like to keep it as a memento of his father. He wonders about sending it to Kate, she would like it, she loves the Bay, it would remind her of walks with David, but then he knows what she would say to him, what she has said to him so many times: 'but where are you, Simon? Where are you? You are invisible. You are always invisible.' Don't send it to Kate, he tells himself. Just for myself then? Maybe the kids, when they are older, except they would ask: 'why are there no photos of you?' He thinks for a moment that maybe he should add a picture of himself, but there are too many reasons why he cannot bring himself to do so.

That afternoon, after two trips to the tip having cleared the dining room and living room, Simon sits back down at the laptop and decides that he will turn the folder into a photo album, all the pages together in one file, the pictures of Ruth and Hannah and Howard and Irene facing the pages of their particular days. He creates a cover, a photograph of David in his sixties, underneath which he has typed: *"Focus!"* and then: *"David Phillips"*. He mails it to a company that turns photos into albums and two days later, a package arrives with the album in it. It looks good. Simon holds it in his hands. He places it on the coffee table in the living room. He leaves it there while he makes a start on clearing the spare room.

That evening, Simon sits on the sofa and looks at the album on the table. He wonders what his father would say about the book. He turns the pages slowly. When he comes to the photograph of Ruth, he says out loud:

"I have added things."

He wonders if David's spirit is there, watching, listening.

"Is that ok?" Simon asks nervously, just in case.

He realises that David might resent his interference, worries suddenly that he has inserted himself inappropriately, that he has turned his father's creation into an unwanted collaboration.

If David's spirit is there, it says nothing, but Simon keeps turning the pages anyway. He stops at the photograph of Hannah, "do you remember?" he asks, "what was she planting?". David would know, he had loved the garden, it is neglected now. When he comes to the four pictures of Howard, he pauses to look at his brother. "Oh Dad," he says, "what was it that made you think of him?" Still no response. And then there is the photograph of Irene. Simon asks David the question he should have asked a long time ago: "what happened?"

He closes the album.

"Well," he says, "I hope that is ok. I hope you are happy with what I have done."

In that instant, he so wants his father to be sat next to him, on the sofa, the album between them. He wants his father to smile with pleasure, to appreciate his efforts. More than anything, he wants David, like he saw him do so many times with Hannah, to place the palm of his hand against his cheek and tell his son that he loves him.

DAVID

When I had finished writing *An Imagined Life,* the book I had written for my mother, and when it became clear that time was now running out for me, I decided to do something that I had meant to do when I finally retired, which was four years ago, even though there is now probably not going to be the time needed to complete the project. Project! Is that what it is? Is that what I need it to be? That is too grand, I think. It is less than a project. A focus. It will be a focus, that will do. I had thought that it might take two months, maybe three, although I had also thought that I would get bored, or lack the required discipline, which is why I didn't start it in the first place. Now I think that if I can manage two months, I would be happy. I don't need to complete it. I am not even sure that I know what completion would be.

So, this is my focus: I walk to the same place every day, overlooking the Bay, a place that I have stopped at so many times over the years, the place that I took my mother, Ruth, to on her visit, a place that gives me great pleasure, great satisfaction. It looks across the mouth of the Kent estuary over to the low profile of Grange on the far shore. I go there at the same time every day and, at exactly the same time, 10.30 in the morning, using my phone, I take a photograph of exactly the same view. It is the same view except that, each day, the view differs slightly from the day before. The light is different, the water sits differently on the sands, red-legged oystercatchers may or may not gather at the water's edge, there may or may not be a shoal of black-tailed godwits skimming the surface, or solitary curlews fishing for worms. And, over time, the view changes more significantly as the tide orchestrates the relationship between land and sea, a love affair, gentle and profound.

Each day, I take a photograph of this view and I say out loud what is uppermost in my mind. When I get home, I upload the photo and transcribe the words that my phone has recorded, words that capture what I am thinking or what I am feeling, thoughts and feelings that have been stimulated by the sights and sounds before me. I am grateful to my phone, where would I be without it? For there to be something so small, so light, so adept, capable of so much more than I am able to appreciate, more than I am willing to learn from my grandchildren, who are so eager to teach me and so disappointed by my lack of interest.

Originally, I had intended my thoughts and feelings to be about the view: the Bay, the sea, the light, the birds - plus perhaps, some memories or musings that it may have evoked in me. And on many days, these are the subject matter of the words that I have recorded and that I transcribe verbatim on my return, below that day's image, a new file to add to the folder I have created on my laptop. But because I am ill, because I am dying, on some days my musings roam beyond the merely descriptive; they are often more reflective. I look at shafts of sunlight searching out patches of blue water amongst the grey, for example, and I find myself remembering the highlights of my life, and then wondering whether there are any more to come in the time that is left to me, and I might say into my phone: '*is there just grey water for me now?*'

Just as the view is subtly different from day to day, and just as the rhythms of the monthly cycle repeat themselves with enduring patience, so I too am subtly different each morning: stronger, weaker, more or less positive, more or less willing to look beyond the view in front of me at the landscape inside of me, more or less able to interpret what I see there, the great expanse of my life, with its own patterns and rhythms, its tidal sweeps and daily alterations, its population not of birds, but of people, so many people.

Standing here, I am witness also to a larger cycle that is taking place in this segment of the Bay, one that I find deeply moving. In the bottom right corner of the photograph that I take each day, it is possible to see a loose collection of clumps of coarse grass. They make little sense where they are unless you understand that they have made their way here from Grange, on the other side of the estuary. They are the vanguard of a migration of the salt marsh from one shore to the other. It is as if some spirit had carefully lifted them from their familiar site, and carried them, one by one, under the cover of darkness, a clump of grass on its base of sandy mud, across the gaping mouth of the estuary, and set them down with equal care in a preordained place, according to a given plan, as if they were pieces in a jigsaw.

It seems miraculous to me that an entire salt marsh can be transposed from one shore to the other over time, influenced by the pull of the deep channels in the Bay as they restlessly resituate themselves in obedience to powers beyond my understanding. They say that this cycle takes place every seventy years or so; that is the age that I will likely be when I die, but the salt marsh does not use time as a measure. It does not need time, it is content with its repeated silent transfer, driven by the currents that reshape the river bed. It is only us humans that need to measure ourselves by time, by the past, present and future. On the days when I am reflective, I think about how I strove to be unencumbered by my particular past, to disconnect from it, divorce myself from it. Now, standing by the low wall where I set my phone camera on its little tripod, looking out across the bay, the tide imperceptibly shifting, channels of water inscribing the moist sands with ancient runes yet to be deciphered, I can see that, like the salt marsh, I just repeat myself, the past folding itself into the present, the future waiting to bear witness, an invisible undertow orchestrating it all. I am powerless in its pull.

I stood here with my mother when she came to visit me. I wanted her to see what I see, to feel what I feel, to share my admiration for the fluid interplay between light, sea and sand; but she didn't look at the view. She was only interested in the past. She showed no interest in the nearly fifty years that I had lived since she had died. No questions. No curiosity. Perhaps she felt that it would be rude to ask, that it was none of her business, or that she had forfeited the right to know. Perhaps she felt that it was her duty, as my mother, to carefully lift my old memories, clump by clotted clump, from the distant shore of the past to the adjacent shore of the present, to carefully position them close enough to each other so that I could imagine the picture that she wanted to show me, the picture of my childhood, a picture of the life I had shared with her.

Perhaps, like all of us, she was only really interested in herself. Perhaps she wanted reassurance, like all of us, that she wasn't quite as bad a parent, a person, as she imagined herself to be. Perhaps she wanted to reestablish an old connection with me, to pick up where she had left off. Or was that me? I had invited her after all. And anyway, my nearly fifty years of lived experience since she died would have been an impassable gulf, separating us from each other yet again, leaving us on opposite shores of the Bay. I was relieved by her lack of curiosity. I had no desire to tell her about my life, I have no desire to tell anyone about my life, why would it be of interest to them, I would get bogged down in detail, they would drift away. What would my mother have made of it? So much has changed in those nearly fifty years, she would have needed footnotes at the bottom of every page. Best for us to stick to what we know, and there was enough we didn't know about that to keep us busy for a weekend at the very least.

One day, cold and grey, I look at the view and I wonder: will my mother be there at my funeral? Will my dead wife? My dead son? My grandfather? My dead friends? I must make sure that there are enough seats for them all, the dear departed. Will I be able to see them there? Of course not. I know that. There will be a smattering of the living and I will not be there to see them either. This desire in us to be present after death, it has caused so much trouble, and yet I feel it now, I berate myself, it is the old grandiosity, the need to be more than just an animal. Look at the salt marsh repositioning itself, it too has its life cycle; it may seem immortal, but there will be changes, the conditions that govern its existence will be affected, there will be a time when it too will cease to be.

Another day, a clear sky, a low tide, gulls strutting on the sand, I think about my father, Charles. Charlie. I wonder if *he* will be at my funeral. If so, he won't want to be there, he didn't like funerals, didn't approve of death. He will be sat near the back, on his own, ready to slip away unnoticed, annoyed with himself for being there, a sign of weakness. I am glad he is there, in spite of everything. He should be there. He has a right to be there. He has a duty to be there. And then, at the end, as people file out, he waits for my mother, Ruth, and as she passes, he steps into the aisle alongside her. She is surprised and then so pleased to see him. He says something to her that makes her laugh, in spite of the occasion, she tilts her head back and then slips her arm through his. They are joined again by their love for each other, and the rest of us watch in wonder, confused by this evidence that their love was true.

I picture my grandfather, Morris: he is watching bereft as Charlie walks his daughter down the aisle, away from him, for the second time. My dear wife notices his distress and comes over to introduce herself, she holds out her hand and says: 'I am David's wife, Hannah.' Morris is glad to be distracted and is delighted to meet the woman his grandson married. I love Hannah, as I always loved her, and in that moment, I love her all over again, just for her empathy: that she would see the old man's distress, that she would want to assuage it, that she would know how to do so.

My living son, Simon, sits on the front row, between his two children, Jess and Tom. He is sad but not sorry that his father is dead. It is a release for us both. His wife, Kate, sits apart from them. She feels bad that she had not made the effort to see me before I died. She had feared my judgement - even though she knew that I would not have been judgemental - so she stayed away. It is a pity that the living and the dead can only interact in my imagination. Howard, my dead son, would like to embrace his living brother, to apologise to him, to seek his forgiveness, which would have been forthcoming. He would like to introduce himself to his niece and nephew. Instead, Howard hovers, uncertain as always, and then his mother beckons to him and he goes over to her and to the old man she is talking to, his father's grandfather he assumes, and Hannah takes his arm and pulls him close to her and they welcome him warmly.

My last photograph: it is surprising how quickly the salt marsh has returned. I feel that it has made an extra effort on my behalf. There are still large gaps to be filled, but the design is clear and the outcome beyond doubt. Soon the migration will be complete, from shore to shining shore. I have forced myself to come here over the last week. 'Just one more day,' I say to myself: 'let's see how you feel,' I reply. It is harder for me to set up the tripod and position the phone. I fumble. My fingers. The words I speak become fewer. There is less to say, and less breath to say it with. Anyway, I have said it all, haven't I? I have said all there is to say, and if there is more, it escapes me. But I always do manage to say something. Something simple. It might be: 'the sky is clear', or 'a lone heron', or 'it is too wet', or 'I am weary'.

This last day is the forty first. Not bad. More than I had thought. Less than I had hoped. It is a dark, grey day, the clouds press like blotting paper on the dank sand. In the distance, black columns of rain drill fiercely down into the sea. In the foreground, there is someone walking towards the cave. It is a young woman, her hair dancing about her head. The wind places the flat of its great hand in the small of her back and propels her urgently forward. If she could, she would fly; instead, she leaves a stammering line of footprints behind her. I decide to wait until she is in shot even though this will be later than my 10.30 deadline. Just as I take the photograph, she catches sight of me and turns and waves, and this simple gesture, and her good nature, and her pleasure in the moment - they break my heart. It is such a long time since I have allowed myself to think of my sister, to think of Irene, and there she is, on the sand, as she might have been, an absence in my life that in that instant, to my surprise, I feel acutely. The woman on the sand shouts something up to me. I am able to raise my hand in response but have no voice with which to call back down to her. She waves again and lets the wind push her out of sight. When I have recovered, when my heart has settled, when my tears have dried, I take the phone from the tripod and say simply: *"my sister"*. The wind is too strong for me and I am too weak for the wind. I struggle to stay on my feet and have to sit down on the bench behind me for a moment with my eyes closed. I think not just of Irene, but of Howard, and of Hannah, and of Ruth and Charlie. I think of my son, Simon. There have been so many absences. I bring the phone back to my mouth and say: *"what fools we have been."*

RUTH

When he first received his diagnosis, when he was told that the tumors were not benign, that there was little that could be done, that decisions needed to be made about how he wanted to proceed, David's thoughts naturally turned to his mother. She had died when he was 23 and when she was 52, and he was now 69, so, to his surprise, it was coming up to fifty years ago. Good grief! He thought that he would like to see her again. He thought: I would like to reach back in time and invite my mother to visit me, for the weekend perhaps. His mother as she was before she died, before she became ill, his mother as he would like to remember her.

What will she see, he wonders, when she sees me? What will it be like for me to see her again? He closes his eyes, looks deep inside himself, into the part of him that is full of memories, a loose jumble of memories now, and he finds her there, and he says to her: "would you like to come and visit me for the weekend?" and Ruth, his mother's name is Ruth, says: "I thought you would never ask."

And now she is sat at his table and he is old enough to be

her father and yet he is still her son. She steals glances at him: he is no longer as skinny as she remembers and he no longer has the thicket of dark curls that she used to like to ruffle with her fingers. He asks her whether her journey has been difficult, whether she needs a rest. She smiles at him, she appreciates the thought, pats him on the arm as she used to do, is pleased to see that he is as considerate of her now as he was as a boy. She shakes her head: she wants to stay close to her son.

Ruth tells him that she is hungry and he brings her some food: rye bread, cheese, olives, a handful of smoked almonds.

She takes some olives.

"I haven't eaten for such a long time," she says.

"Of course," says David.

He watches her as she savours the cheese, the bread, the nuts. She is as he remembers her, as she is in the photograph that sits on his desk. She is in her forties, handsome, her hair is as she had it then, short and dyed a strawberry blonde.

"Was I a good mother?" Ruth asks, suddenly.

"Goodness," David says. "Goodness."

She looks at him. This is yes or no. He has to think about it? Why can't he give her an answer?

Instead, he says: "do *you* think you were?"

Maybe all she wanted was to answer her own question. What would she do with his answer anyway? Would she believe him? If you have to ask the question, you already know the answer.

"I died. That's never good," she says.

He looks at her.

"Before you died?"

"Who am I to say?"

Who is she to say? He remembers when he was ill as a child, struggling to breathe, how she would soothe him. He remembers that she would buy his favourite biscuits, chocolate digestives. He remembers peeling potatoes for her in the kitchen, the two of them at the table. He remembers how she would place the palm of her hand against his cheek sometimes, and smile at him. Would it help to share these memories with her?

David laughs. "Well, here I am," he says. "Do I look like the son of a good mother?"

Ruth studies him. She is curious.

"I didn't think you would lose your hair like that. Your father kept his hair. My father kept his hair."

"That's not your fault."

"And your paunch."

"Did you always focus on the negative?"

"Always."

David laughs again. It is true. He remembers. She used to focus on the negative.

The following morning, David suggests that they go for a walk.

"Come for a walk with me," he says.

Ruth looks at him reproachfully.

"I don't walk."

"What do you mean, you don't walk?"

"I don't understand how you live like this."

She means in the country, like this, so far from everything. It is like a Venetian not living in Venice. Why? Why do that to yourself? She looks out of the window: there is nothing there. Fields. Grass. Trees. She will not look more closely.

"I had to get away," he explains.

"That I understand. But here?"

Yesterday it had rained, it had been cold. He had found a fleece for her to wear.

"I had to get away from everything."

"Everything," she says.

She thinks: what is everything? was it so bad? Clearly it was. Did she know how bad it was? Such a long time ago, how is she expected to remember?

David finds her some walking boots. "Really?" she says. She puts them on, why not, what's the worst that can happen? 'I'll tell you what's the worst that can happen,' she used to say, 'then you'll be sorry'. There was always this wagging finger in her voice. Was it so bad? She looks at him. He wants to go for a walk, to show her what? Fields? Trees? Sheep?

He takes her on his *if there's time in the day and it's not too wet* walk. From the house, they cross the road and over a stile onto a path that leads through a wood. Shafts of light land on moss and stone. It is muddy, and she thinks: does he want me to slip in the mud? They reach the water meadow. He tells her that in early summer it is covered with wild flowers. She smiles at him, unconvinced. They splash their way to the gate on the far side of the meadow. Through the gate, they climb up to what was once a duck pond. Ruth is short of breath. "What are you trying to do to me?"

They pause. The pond is overgrown now. He tells her that there is no space for the ducks to land any more.

"I know how they feel," Ruth says.

David laughs.

"No you don't," he says.

They walk across a field for a while in silence. He points to a large rock that seems to rise up out of the ground.

"My boys used to climb that rock when they were small. They used to race each other. Howard would always win." He laughs.

His boys, she thinks. My grandsons.

They cross a road and enter into Eaves Wood.

"I have some questions for you," he tells her.

Of course he has. She feels calm suddenly.

"You have some questions for me?"

"I do," he says.

"You bring me into this wilderness so that you can ask me questions?"

"Wilderness!"

He laughs. They laugh.

They are walking up a gentle incline with the wood to the right of them and views across fields to the village on their left.

"There's our house," David points it out to her.

He said 'our', Ruth doesn't question it. She thinks how much she prefers inside to outside.

"So ask," she says.

They walk on a little more before he says:

"Were you angry with me?"

She thinks for a moment: what if I say yes?

"No, I wasn't angry with you," she says.

He looks at her, unconvinced.

"You know when I mean?"

"I know when you mean. The phone call."

"I put the phone down on him. I made it worse. Worse for you."

"I told him he was being unreasonable."

He looks at her again, surprised.

"What did he say?"

He remembers, once, when he thought that his father was going to hit him, when his anger had broken loose of its moorings, his mother had put her body between them, held them apart, pushing with her palms against their chests. He remembers thinking: go on! hit me, finally. It would have been a relief. It had been brave of her.

One of Ruth's laces has come undone and she bends down to retie it. She says sharply:

"He didn't hit me. I want you to know that."

"Ok."

"He shouted at me. He shouted: 'you always take his side!'"

David looks at her, curious.

"Did you?" he asks.

"What?" She is puzzled.

"Always take my side?"

She sighs. "I did my best. It wasn't easy."

They walk downhill now and between some houses to a road that leads to the shore. They sit on a bench near the entrance to a small cave which looks like a bullet hole that has been shot into the cliff face.

"I heard him shout that at you once," David decides to tell his mother.

Ruth is startled. "When?"

"Not long before you died. You were at home, in bed. He wanted you to have a blood transfusion, in hospital, and I disagreed. He was angry with me, you must have tried to calm him down, and he screamed at you. I was shocked."

"He was frightened. He couldn't admit that I was dying. He took it personally."

"You always take his side," says David gently, smiling.

"What was I supposed to do?" Ruth looks at him in despair. "I loved him."

They walk on, climb a short rise and sit on another bench with a view over the whole expanse of the Bay. The tide is out. He expects me to admire the view, she thinks, but to her it is just more mud, taupe under a grey sky. She stands up, impatient, and they follow the path to some fields.

Ruth turns to him. "What were you doing in the house?"

He stops and looks out at the shore, stretching to the horizon, abandoned by the sea.

"Do you not remember me being there?"

"You couldn't have been there. He wouldn't have allowed it."

She loses her footing - she can see Charlie's face - and David takes her arm to steady her.

"I wrote to him," he explains.

"You wrote to him?" Ruth is astonished.

"Grandpa told me to. He insisted. For your sake."

"You didn't want to?"

"I was angry."

"But you wrote to him?" she says it again to make sure.

"I wanted to see you. I wanted to be with you."

"And Charlie agreed?"

"Reluctantly."

"It would have been difficult for him," she says.

David shakes his head.

They walk across a field and through a stile.

"One day, when I was at the house," David says, "when you were dying, I was sat by your bed, you were asleep most of the time by then, and suddenly you sat up, bolt upright, and gave this great sob and you cried out: 'forgive me, mummy, forgive me.'"

Ruth is silent for a moment.

"What did you do?" the mother asks her son.

"I tried to comfort you. You were inconsolable."

"You shouldn't have had to see these things."

"It was fine. I was ok." He tries to reassure her.

They walk on.

"Why did you want forgiveness?" he asks.

"I have no idea," Ruth says quickly.

David looks at her quizzically, but says nothing.

Ruth stops for a moment and looks out over the bay.

"My mother died when I was thirteen years old. I had been evacuated because of the blitz, and when I came back, she was dead."

"Jesus."

"So you see, death runs in the family."

He shakes his head.

"I lived alone with my father. Seven, eight years. It is a long time."

"The photo I have of you both," he says, "have you seen it on the wall? Some kind of formal dinner. You look beautiful. You are sat next to grandpa and you are leaning towards him, and he is leaning towards you, your shoulders are touching, and you look so happy, both of you."

"We were happy. We loved each other. We lived together." She sounds angry with him.

They walk in silence for a while.

"He told me that I had to marry."

"He made you marry my father?"

"Charlie was so handsome. It was just after the war. He had such good teeth. And he made me laugh. Morris didn't *make* me marry him. I knew that there was another life for me to live."

Ruth stops walking. The sun, out again, is sliding towards the horizon, the tide is turning and the sea starts to make its long way back to the shore. There are cows mooching around in this field. They chew some grass, they look up, they see the mother and her son standing there and they think: what are these animals that don't eat grass? They bend their heads back down to the ground. Ruth breathes deeply, as if she is breathing memories not air, in, out, in, out.

"How much further?" she asks.

David laughs. "Miles."

"Why does he do this to me? My own son?" she says and he laughs, and she laughs, and they walk arm in arm to the rough gate that leads to the road back to the village.

She brings mud into the hallway.

"Look," she says, as if it is his fault.

"It's ok." He fetches a dustpan and brush.

Ruth takes off the boots and hands them to him. She

doesn't ask whom they belong to. He would have told her if he had wanted her to know.

David lights the fire in the grate and sits his mother in front of it and goes to make a pot of tea. She likes this house, her son's home. She likes this room, the walls are a soft white, the light comes easily through the windows, the fire gives off warmth, the chair she sits in holds her well. There is a curved vase on a window sill holding dried flower heads, Ruth wishes she knew their name. There are rugs on the floor and pictures on the walls. Everything feels like it has its story, that it means something to somebody, that it has found its place. One picture, it makes no sense to her at first, broad bands of colour, greens and browns crossed by thin vertical stripes of yellow and white, she finds it quite beautiful without knowing why. Are the bands fields? Are the stripes trees? The top band is orange and she realises that this might be a sunset, the simple telling of an evening sky suffused with a gathering glory. She thinks of the house in Stanmore, how different it was. The pictures on the walls there meant nothing to her, Charlie chose them. She wonders if they mean anything to him. The Hay Wain over the fireplace in the lounge. It was just there, filling a void. She never looked at it. She couldn't remember how it got there, nor what story held it there.

David comes back with the tea. He places a tray on the table between them and pours her a cup and offers her a plate of biscuits. Chocolate digestives. Ruth takes one.

"Did you?" she asks. "Get away from everything?"

He sits facing her on the sofa.

"I tried to make some kind of peace with Charlie. We were in the house together for, I don't know, two weeks, maybe three. After your funeral, he disappeared, I never heard from him again, didn't know where he was, nothing."

She shakes her head.

"I put it behind me," David says. "I started again."

"You never leave it all behind," she says.

"Even unto death?" he asks. "Even unto death."

The next day, the Sunday, it is raining and Ruth is pleased.

"I'm not walking in this," she says.

David smiles at her.

"What *do* you want to do?"

"I want to cook for you."

He has to sit down. He has to stop himself from crying.

"What do you want to cook?"

She is already looking through the fridge, his cupboards.

"We can go shopping," he says, "or make a list, I can go shopping."

They sit together at the kitchen table.

"I remember," he says, "grandpa would come round during the day sometimes, when dad was at the shop, and you would make lunch for him and you would discuss the price of things, bread, milk, eggs, coffee, how much they had gone up. Always up."

"What else is there to talk about?" she asks.

What else? David thinks.

"Don't ask me the price of anything," he says.

"You don't need to know?"

"I'm lucky."

He has another memory, should he share it with her? Some Sundays, they would have lunch together, the two of them, before his father got back from the shop. He didn't get back until mid-afternoon, the shop was in the East End, he closed at two, it was at least an hour's drive depending on the traffic and so they would eat together, mother and son, at the kitchen table, a moment of sweet companionship, a moment of peace before he returned. He remembered specifically: chicken and rice.

"Do you remember," David says, "you used to cook chicken and rice, on a Sunday. I used to love that."

Ruth doesn't remember.

"If you say so," she says.

"I'm sure," he says.

"It was good?"

"Very good."

She smiles.

There are some chicken pieces in the fridge. There is rice in the cupboard. Ruth does what she can with what is available. They sit and eat together at the kitchen table.

"Not as good," she says.

"I thought you didn't remember?"

Ruth shrugs.

"It tastes good to me," he says.

"Seasoned with memories."

"Is that a saying?" he asks.

Later, David finds her standing in front of the photograph of her and her father at the formal dinner.

"I was beautiful," she says. Her hair was a chestnut brown then.

"You were."

"You forget."

They look so happy, father and daughter, they look like man and wife, like it could be their wedding feast.

"Do you remember?" he asks her gently.

She shakes her head.

When it is time for her to go, they stand facing each other and David takes his mother's hands.

"Thank you for coming," he says.

"Thank you for inviting me."

"Do you know, I don't think I ever grieved properly, for you."

"You were busy," she excuses him.

"Even so."

Ruth looks at her son, places the palm of her hand against his cheek.

"Ach, grief," she says "it is not all that it is cracked up to be."

He laughs.

And with that she is gone.

David sits at the kitchen table, suddenly deflated. There is no sign of the meal his mother cooked for him, no plates scraped clean, no trace of her. He is left alone with his memories. He curls forward in his chair. It is as if his mother has taken the bulk of him away with her and left just a husk. This will not do, he thinks. He breathes deeply, reflating himself so that he is able to sit up straight and focus his eyes again. I need something, he thinks. I need something to do. He wonders at how little he knew about his mother's life, about how they had never had the chance to fill in the blanks, and about how her visit has raised more questions than answers. He decides, there and then, alone at the table in the kitchen, in the space left by her departure, that he will write his mother's story, a version of her story. He will fill in the blanks himself. He will write it just for her. He will call it '*An Imagined Life.*'

PART II

AN IMAGINED LIFE

THE BALL

When Ruth is nineteen years old, her father, Morris, invites her to accompany him to the annual ball of his Masonic Lodge, of which this year he is the Master. She of course accepts his invitation. Ruth is of an age when strangers, catching sight of them together in the street, father and daughter, walking arm in arm as they sometimes do, might assume that they are husband and wife. Morris looks younger than his years and Ruth looks older, the difference in age seems unremarkable. They make a handsome couple. There is nothing in her face to suggest that she might be related to him, she has her mother's looks, thank goodness, and she thinks that their life together, their relationship to each other, although it is by no means that of a husband and wife, is also somehow more than that of a father and daughter.

With her father's help, Ruth chooses a dress from her mother's wardrobe, still full of her clothes, and a necklace from the box on the dressing table. She adds the white fur stole that she used to dress up in as a child, pretending that she was a queen, or a princess. Morris has bought her a pair of earrings for the occasion. He looks at his daughter when she presents herself to him: what does he see, *who* does he see? In that dress, it could be Rachel, he has to remind himself that this is Ruth, this is his daughter, that his wife is dead, that she has not come back to life, that the hole that she has left has not been filled, that he must not be taken in by this mirage. He tells Ruth that she is beautiful, that she looks magnificent, a princess, no, a queen, and he offers her his arm and leads her through the apartment to the stairs and down to the waiting taxi.

She slides her arm through his as they walk down the middle of the room to their places at the top table. They are an irresistible force parting the crowd, who step back to admire them. Morris and Ruth take their seats and once they do so others are able to take theirs. For Ruth this is magical: it is as if she is both wife and daughter at the same time, it is her ideal, and Ruth wishes that the moment could last forever, that the dinner was in fact a ceremony that made permanent this double contract. She does not want to turn back into only the daughter at the end of the evening. Before the food is served, the photographer sets up his camera. "Just the two of you," he says and Ruth instinctively leans in against her father, her shoulder touching his.

"Yes!" says the photographer, and he captures this moment of intimacy. "Perfect!"

They are first onto the dance floor, once the dishes of apple pie and ice cream have been cleared away and the tables have been pushed back to the sides of the room. Morris is a fine dancer, upright, fluid, elegant, in rhythm with the music. He places his hand on Ruth's waist and she places her hand on his shoulder and he takes her other hand in his and they float across the floor, barely touching it, and the other couples watch and wait, reluctant to intrude. There is a ripple of applause and then they become one pair among many. Ruth rests her head on her father's chest, listening for the beat of his heart.

She has never been happier, never felt more fulfilled. She holds at bay the knowledge that this is make-believe.

After that first dance, they separate. Morris must circulate whilst Ruth must dance with a queue of men eager to imagine that they are young again. When it is possible, she withdraws to a chair by the wall to rest. She is tired suddenly. As she catches her breath, she realises that she is out of place here, she is a daughter not a wife, she is just a nineteen-year-old girl, she is a substitute. She wonders whether her desire to be her father's wife might in fact be a longing for her mother. Perhaps it is simply that, without ever admitting it, she misses her mother so profoundly that she wants to become her, as if by becoming her she is bringing her back to life, as if by becoming her she will be able to once again be a mother to her daughter, and her daughter, herself, Ruth, who has never gone away, who is still alive, who is here now, will be able to receive this mothering even as she, Ruth, as her mother, is providing it. These thoughts are dizzying and they make her sad. For a second, she allows herself to imagine being mothered. She remembers, before the war, Rachel in her apron, standing in the doorway, shouting her name, that simple act, calling her in from the street. How she wishes that her mother was here now, sat beside her, holding her hand, talking to her. Ruth goes to the Ladies room to powder her nose.

The last time Ruth had seen her mother was through the window of the train that was taking her away, taking her into exile. She was angry and refused to look at Rachel through the smoke-stained glass. She had told her mother several times that she was too old to be evacuated, she was eleven years old, that she didn't want to go away, didn't want to be separated from her parents, that this was more frightening for her than any bomb, that she would go to the shelters, she was not stupid, she would be safer with them than with strangers, couldn't she see? how could she be so cruel? how could she separate her from her father? she couldn't bear it. She was determined not to cry, to look straight ahead as she felt the train gather its strength, not to turn even when she realised that the train had already started to move slowly forward. She sensed her mother moving too, along the platform, in her uniform, she hoped that her mother was crying, let her cry, it's her fault. Ruth didn't turn, didn't cry, she sat like stone, she was disbelieving. She couldn't imagine what would happen next.

When it was time to return, she dreaded coming back to the absence of her mother, to the thought that it would be her father waiting on the platform, a final confirmation of her loss. When Morris had written to her with the news of her mother's death, she did not believe him at first and wondered why he would lie to her in this way: was it to punish her? Then she was stricken, her grief swallowed her whole, she was held captive by it with no hope of release. On the train back to London, in anticipation of the life awaiting her, Ruth became angry, as angry as she was when she had left. It was obvious to her that if she had not been sent away, Rachel would not have died, that the bomb would not have fallen, that the daughter's very presence would have kept the mother alive. It was Rachel's fault for sending her away and Ruth blamed her for everything. She vowed then that she would never forgive her mother.

Her father was waiting on the platform, handsome in his camel hair coat and his trilby. Morris had once told her that the coat smelled of camel and she had believed him. He had told her that he had fought with the camel corps in the desert in the last war and she had asked him if that was where he had got the coat and he had looked at her and said yes. He had told her that he had had the coat made from the hair of his camel after it had been shot from under him by a German sniper. Ruth had believed him. Morris had told her that if she pressed her nose to the coat, she would find the smell of camel. She had tried. 'What does camel smell like?' she had asked. 'Hot sand,' he had said. She was pleased to see the coat again and pleased to see her father whom she now felt that she barely knew. She remembered how heavy the coat was and wondered whether, after her time in the country, she would be able to lift it now.

Morris picked up her small cardboard suitcase and taking his daughter's hand, led her through the throng at the station to a café where he bought her a lemonade. She didn't say anything, she didn't cry, she didn't look at her father, she sipped her drink, she sat like stone. Morris, who had himself only recently found a way back to his composure, seeing Ruth again, Rachel's daughter, became reacquainted with his grief. It took time for him to quell the surge of feeling. Whilst he stilled his heart, he watched Ruth, he waited, he wondered what she might be thinking and what he might say that would be of any help to her. Eventually, he reached out his hand:

"Well, it is just the two of us now."

She took his hand:

"Yes."

Ruth didn't go back to school. For a start, the school wasn't there anymore, it was a space filled with rubble, but also, she had never liked going to school, was no good at schoolwork, was not clever in that way. And besides, she had her father to look after. He had brought what was left of their belongings to a new apartment, the second floor of a house in Shoreditch, and she did what she could to make a home for them both there. He gave her his coupons and she queued and tried, sometimes successfully, to charm extra from the butcher and the grocer. None of Rachel's recipe books had survived the bombing, but Ruth could remember some of the dishes that her mother used to make and she taught herself how to cook them. Her father was always complimentary, he seemed to enjoy what she set before him.

It is now six years since she returned and, in that time, Ruth has become a housewife. She shops, she cooks, she cleans, she launders. She makes Morris his breakfast in the mornings, a bowl of prunes and a cup of coffee, and a sandwich for his lunch, and as he leaves, she calls out to him cheerfully, "have a good day!" Then she sits and has her cup of coffee and a slice of toast and margarine and plans what she will do next. She might babysit for Beth on the first floor or she might keep Judith company on the third. If it is fine, she might take Beth's baby in her pram to the little park. Then she carries out her chores. She shops for the evening meal and also for Judith, who is not able to get out now, she shouldn't be on the third floor, but what can she do? Morris comes back in time for supper; they sit and eat the rollmop that he has brought back with him, the casserole that she has made, they will discuss the prices in the shops, he will tell her stories about his brothers or about the secretary in the office or a difficult customer, he will eat an apple with a slice of cheese. She will set aside a portion of the casserole to take to Judith the next day.

Ruth is happy. She likes being a housewife, even though she is not a wife. Beth sometimes makes a joke about her being in no-man's-land, and this upsets Ruth, because she loves her father and cannot imagine not living with him, not looking after him, and more, she does not want him to be on his own, not again. Judith tells Ruth that she must think of herself, that she must not devote her life to Morris, that she is not responsible for his happiness. Her two neighbours think that Morris is taking advantage of her daughterly love, but she knows this not to be the case, even though, as Beth says, he is not exactly looking for a wife. It is true that he does not seem to be seeking a relationship with another woman, though she is not sure whether she would know if he was and has wondered lately whether this is a subject that she should raise with him, and then realises that this would feel inappropriate and then wonders why and asks herself: '*is* it inappropriate?' Does he feel obliged to stay single for her sake? How would she feel if he announced that there *was* another woman in his life? Would she be hurt? Would she feel relieved?

Every Friday, Morris' two surviving brothers come to dinner. They are all that is left of a once sprawling family. She boils a chicken for them. She serves them the broth with noodles and then chopped liver on matzah with sliced cucumber, then the breast of the chicken with potatoes and carrots, then Sol's favourite, lokshen pudding, bought not made. She sits and listens to these three Jews as they eat their soup noisily, venerating the past, bemoaning the present, catastrophising the future. They say their prayers for the dead: there are so many. She likes to hear them as they talk business, they run the family business, she is interested. They agree to send her to secretarial college so that she can work in the office on Commercial Street - 'if she types as well as she cooks,' they say and smile at her. She is pleased.

She had thought it best to not think about her mother, not to miss her, not to remember her. She is not angry with her any more, she knows that that was foolish, but still she has not forgiven her. Morris and her uncles want to remember the dead, to honour them, to keep them close, how can they bear it? she cannot bear it, they have so many more memories than her, to fetch out her memories of her mother now, to lay them out like jewels on her dressing table – what good would this do? She thought it best to leave them hidden and over time to forget where she had hidden them.

After the ball, Ruth takes off the necklace and places it carefully in her mother's jewellery box and hangs the dress and the stole back in the wardrobe. She is not her mother. She is not her father's wife, she will not live with him forever, it had been a magical evening, make-believe, that is all. She puts on her dressing gown and goes to her father, who is sitting in his chair in the living room, sipping a whiskey, and she says to him:

"Thank you for a lovely evening."

"My dear girl," Morris says.

She unhooks the earrings and holds them in her hand.

"I was very proud of you tonight," he says.

"Thank you."

"You remind me so much of your mother."

She smiles at him.

"I'm glad," she says.

She kisses him on the cheek and says good night.

After she has gone to bed, Morris sits for a while, nursing his whiskey. This will not do. The eldest brother, Sol, had growled this at him as he left the flat one Friday evening: 'this will not do.' When they were dancing, when Ruth had laid her head on his chest, he could feel himself enveloped in a mist of confusion. For a moment he was not certain who he was dancing with, surely this was Rachel, his wife, returned to him, taking her rightful place in his arms, and he had felt such joy in that instant and then such pain as the instant passed. He had managed to keep dancing, even though it was no longer Rachel in his arms.

It was not fair to Ruth to use her in this way, it had been a mistake to invite her to the ball, he felt foolish. Sol was right: this will not do. By the time the dance was over, he had resolved to clear a space between his daughter and himself. He had resolved to relieve her of any obligation she may feel to take her mother's place, to act the part of his wife. He is her father. She is his daughter. She is not his dead wife, she is not her dead mother, she is a beautiful young woman with her life ahead of her and he must set his own needs, his own fears, to one side.

Morris knows that they cannot continue to live together like this for much longer, that he must not block her path. She must marry. He thinks how this will be, what shape his life will take. His dear wife and her reincarnation, his dear daughter, to lose them both, he has been afraid to feel the full pain of the loss of his wife, he has held it at bay, and now, if he lets Ruth go, it will sweep over him, it will threaten to wash him away. Yet he will survive. He has survived so much, what is one more death to overcome? This will not do. He must set her free.

THE SHOP

ON THE DAYS when Morris is working in the office, he insists on Ruth walking with him from their flat in Shoreditch down to Commercial Street, twenty minutes, at his pace. In these years soon after the war, London is still smouldering. They walk past ruins, mounds of brick and dust, tears in the fabric, spaces once filled with life, empty now and picked over. A soft breeze can still stir smoke from amidst a pile of debris, a wind can rekindle flames, the sour smell of burning there always, you walk past, you don't look, you don't think, you walk past. Ruth, head down, inured, walking at her father's pace, what is to be done after all? It is a relief to get to the office and the sweet smell of Jean's cigarettes.

One of the brothers at least is usually there, sometimes all three of them, sometimes it is just the two secretaries, Ruth and Jean. They enjoy those days together best, free to gossip, Jean has all the gossip, and a way of gossiping, they laugh a lot, it is good for Ruth to laugh like this, though she is not Jean and never could be. Jean asks her about the brothers, about Morris, who is so proper, and Danny who is so improper, and Sol who is so forbidding. They are both scared of Sol; Morris and Danny are scared of Sol, the eldest, the firstborn and foremost. In fact, Ruth knows little about any of them, they don't talk about themselves or much about their past, except to say prayers for the dead. Jean, who has worked for the brothers for years now, at least three years, she can't remember exactly, knows more. Jean likes Morris the best and Ruth is pleased and a little jealous.

"If I was to marry any of them," says Jean, "I would marry Morris."

"Why don't you then?" says Ruth, tartly.

Jean pulls a face.

"What?"

"Too old," she says.

It is Ruth's job to fetch lunch for whoever is in the office, if they want something. Danny usually takes himself down to The Duchess of Alice and comes back humming Irish tunes with the coal-tar smell of Guinness on his breath and they wonder if he has eaten anything at all. Morris, if he is feeling pleased with himself, might take himself to Blooms for salt beef and latkes with hot mustard. Today, Sol, who is in most Fridays, wants bagels and lox to eat in and so Ruth walks from the office on Commercial Street to the delicatessen on Wentworth Street, twelve minutes, at her pace, with its barrels of herring and cucumber, so many different kinds of cucumber, who knew, to buy bagels for Sol, and for Jean and herself, Sol is buying, so why not? She gets the bagels from the old woman shrouded in steam from her kiosk on the corner and takes them still warm to Izzie's and he fills them for her with cream cheese and smoked salmon and chopped onion and capers, a squeeze of lemon and a twist of pepper.

She likes Wentworth Street. It is a street for people, not cars. On one side are the schmutter shops, the tailors standing in the doorways in their waistcoats, tape measures around their necks, their bolts of cloth on trestles on the pavement, they talk to each other, shout insults across the street, make confessions, tell stories, customers would be an interruption, an inconvenience. On the other side, different kinds of shop, a shoe shop, a fishmonger's, a lighting shop. When the wind blows from the wrong direction you can smell the chicken abattoir two streets back, where the blood flows in the gutter and you don't wear your good shoes. Not today though. A young man stands in the doorway of the lighting shop and watches her as she walks by. He is still there when she comes back, clutching her bag of bagels and some rollmops for this evening, and yes, some sweet cucumber and gefilte fish and chrain, why not, they can afford it. He shouts out at her: "give us a bagel, love!" She smiles in spite of herself. She notices that he has good teeth.

The following Friday, as she walks past, he shouts out "Ruthie!". She ignores him. How does he know her name? Izzie at the delicatessen will have told him, Izzie who looks at her in a way she knows she shouldn't like. "Come on Ruthie!" When she walks back with the bag of bagels - she had said no to Izzie this time when he tried to sell her some fresh chopped liver - she is on the other side of the street, squeezing between the tailors and their bolts of cloth. She tries hard not to look to see if he is watching her.

Next Friday, she considers telling Sol that she will go to Bloom's to fetch hot tongue on rye for him, for a change, but before she can, he asks them if they fancy some lokshen pudding and Jean says "ooh, yes please, Sol," and Izzie does the best lokshen pudding, so as she walks down Commercial Street she is thinking: which side of Wentworth Street do I choose?

He is waiting for her when she passes the lighting shop. He steps out in front of her.

"Ruthie, seriously, I need you to do me a favour."

She stops to look at him, takes a step back.

"Ruthie," he says, "seriously, I can't leave the shop, I'm on my own here, get me a bagel would you, I'm starving, I'm dying of hunger! I have the money, here," he holds out some notes, "lox," he says, "please, tell Izzie it's for Charlie, he knows how I like it, no capers, will you?" he takes her hand to press the notes on her, "that's it, Ruthie, you'd be doing me a big favour."

She takes the money.

"It's Ruth," she says.

"Aw, Ruthie, don't be like that. You're an angel." He smiles that big smile, good teeth, set in a handsome face under a cap of curly hair.

"No capers!" he shouts after her.

When she gets back to the office, Jean says to her:

"What's this about you and Charlie Podolski?"

"What do you mean?" She blushes.

Jean laughs her dirty, smoker's laugh.

"He's going to marry you apparently."

Ruth snorts in disbelief.

"Eat your pudding," she says, "you wanted pudding, eat it," as if this were all Jean's fault.

He is a Pole. Normally, Poles ... Danny tells a joke about why Poles have round shoulders and flat foreheads, but Charlie is broad-shouldered, square-faced, he is handsome, his smile is, what? There is something about his smile. His smile makes her want to smile. He is fun, and apart from Jean, there is not much fun in Ruth's life.

"*I* would marry him," says Jean.

"You would marry anybody."

"Anybody," agrees Jean. "But he owns the shop."

"No!" says Ruth.

"True."

"How?"

"It's a mystery."

"Jean!"

"There's a story, I don't know, his grandfather left it to him instead of the father, that's what they say, I don't know, there's a story, that's all I know."

If Jean knew more, she would tell her.

"I'll tell you this," says Jean.

"What?"

"He doesn't ask me to buy his lox for him."

Ruth laughs in spite of herself.

"What are you two laughing about?" says Sol, as he hands Jean a letter to type.

"It's the lokshen pudding, Sol," Jean says, "you shouldn't have. It's made us giddy."

"I knew it," he says, shaking his head sadly and retreating back into his office.

Sunday is market day on Wentworth Street and somehow even more people are packed into the narrow road, with stalls in the gutters and no room to move, fruit stalls and vegetable stalls and junk stalls and noise, noise everywhere, a swell of noise, shouting, laughing, haggling, cries of outrage, greetings and farewells, always the insults and always the kvetching. Ruth forces her way down the street this Sunday, some weeks later, people shouting out to her, asking after Morris, or the business, or the whereabouts of Jean, they make her laugh, they want to make her laugh because she is so serious normally and because she is beautiful when she laughs, even more beautiful. This Sunday, Charlie has asked her if she could help him out, it's his busy day and Jeff, his usual, has let him down. She knows it is a ploy, but she is looking forward to spending time with him and she is curious about the shop and, besides, he has promised to take her to Blooms after, and she has never been.

She pushes through the crowd into the shop, where Charlie is serving a customer, he is on his own, like he said he would be.

He looks up and sees her. His face lights up. When the customer has left - "I'll think about it, Charlie, I promise," - he takes her to a counter at the back, behind which there are racks of light bulbs, so many different kinds, who knew, a whole wall of them and below the counter, shelves full of batteries, again, so many different kinds, she marvels at the complexity of the world, how it has come to pass that there is a need for such a variety of bulbs and batteries, wouldn't it just be simpler to have maybe three or four, how is she going to know which is the right bulb, or the right battery, and then Charlie shows her the drawer where the fuses are kept, again, so many different ones, part of her wants to turn and leave, there is too much for her to learn, she will never remember all this.

"What shall I do?" she asks him.

"I want you to stand here," he brings her to the centre of the shop, so that she can be seen from the doorway. "I want you to stand here, so that people can see you, and they will think who is this beauty and they will come into the shop to find out, you will be my siren, Ruthie, they will come in and when they realise that you are not for sale they will look around and they will see these and these and they will think, if I can't buy Ruthie to light up my life then at least I can buy one of these, it is a poor substitute, but it will be something. Then I will come over and I will deal with them, don't worry."

Ruth shakes her head and rolls her eyes and laughs in spite of herself. He leaves her and stands in the doorway and shouts at the stallholder in front of the shop that he is blocking the way, that his customers are complaining that they can't get through.

Ruth looks at the light fittings fixed to the walls and hanging from the ceilings. It is not a big shop, nor, she notices, is it a clean shop, it is grubby, but it is a bright shop, because all of these lights are shining. The fittings on the wall are half chandeliers, a veil of strings of glass droplets hanging from semicircular brass frames, single frames, doubles, triples, and behind the veils one or more bulbs, she sees that they are all shaped like candles, clear glass. The fittings hanging from the ceiling are full chandeliers, the light refracting from the prism of the glass droplets, glints of colour, it is quite magical. She finds a feather duster in the tiny office, no more than a cupboard really, near the counter at the rear of the shop, and she makes herself busy by dusting the light fittings, the droplets wriggling with pleasure from this unaccustomed attention. Charlie turns and smiles at her, his attention drawn by the tinkling of the glass.

A customer makes their way to the counter and Ruth follows them, putting the feather duster back in the office. They have brought with them the type of bulb they want to buy, it is the one that stopped working. They shake it so that she can hear the broken filament and they show her where the glass has gone black to prove to her that they are not being frivolous. She inspects the bulb to find the information that she needs: it is 60 watts, BC, pearl, shaped like a mushroom, and looks in the racks until she finds a match. The customer waits patiently, happy to watch this lovely creature even if she is taking a long time, what's the hurry? They had thought they would just buy the one bulb to replace the one that has gone, but she is right when she asks them how many they would like, she makes a good point, and they buy two or three, why not, this way when they have to replace the next bulb that goes, they won't have to sit in the dark like they did this time for three days, they exaggerate. Ruth makes a note of the sale in the stock book like Charlie asked her to. It is her first sale.

An old woman comes with her wireless set, a big box of a thing that she fetches out of her carrier bag and puts down on the counter expectantly. Ruth looks at her.

"What can I do for you?" she asks.

"It's the battery."

Ruth finds a screwdriver and unscrews the panel at the back of the wireless. There is a big solid block of a battery there.

"Are you sure it is flat?" she asks.

"Test it for me," says the old woman.

Charlie appears and scolds the customer: "we don't test and we don't fit, stop wasting our time, you want a new battery, you don't, which is it?"

The woman cowers but says nothing.

"Fine," says Charlie and turns away, exasperated.

"Has it stopped working?" asks Ruth.

The old woman nods miserably.

Ruth pulls the old battery out from the back of the wireless and disconnects it. She finds a replacement and works out which wire goes where and how to get the new battery into the set. She screws the panel into place and then says:

"Why don't you switch it on?"

The wireless works. The old woman says nothing, doesn't smile or look at Ruth, she puts the wireless back in her carrier bag.

"How much?" she asks.

Ruth tells her. The old woman pours a scramble of coins out of her purse and Ruth picks out the right amount and pushes the rest back towards her. She scoops the change back into her purse and scuttles away. Ruth makes a note of the sale in the book. Charlie comes back to the counter.

"Time wasters," he spits out angrily. "Time wasters."

On Monday, Ruth tells Jean about Charlie and the old woman.

"There was no need, Jean," she says.

Jean is typing a letter for Danny and she looks at Ruth but says nothing.

"We weren't busy."

"It's the principle," says Jean.

"Principle!" snorts Ruth. "He was horrible to her. There was no need for it."

Jean is checking the letter for errors.

"Maybe he doesn't like old women," she says.

"Maybe he doesn't like Jews," says Ruth, this is what she had wondered.

"Don't be silly, Ruthie!" Jean rolls her eyes. "*He's* a Jew. How could he not like himself?"

Charlie will not invite his father to the wedding. Ruth is shocked. She has never met the father, any of Charlie's family, his mother is dead, she knows that. He won't have it. She says: 'but surely?' and stops because his face clenches shut, she doesn't recognise him. 'Charlie,' she tries and his face turns to rock, she comes to think of it as his rock face; the Charlie she knows has gone somewhere else and left this statue in his place, hard as granite.

She says to Jean:

"What should I do? It's not right, Jean, is it?"

"Who is to say what is right?" says Jean.

"To not talk about it. To not tell me."

"Something happened, Ruthie, that's all I know. Between them, I don't know what, I don't know why, it happened, and now they don't speak, father and son, just like that, I don't know who, whether it was one or the other or both at the same time. Something to do with the shop, I don't know what, don't ask me, it happened, that's all there is. The grandfather's the same, he is old school, he is a hard man."

"Can it be that bad? That bad that not even a wedding ..." Ruth tails off.

"That's what he's telling you. It's that bad."

"He's not telling me anything."

"Yes he is, you are not listening."

"So what, I do nothing, I don't meet my father-in-law, he is as good as dead to me?"

"Ruthie, if you want to make peace, go and work for the United Nations."

"I will," says Ruth, "just to get away from you."

Morris walks her down the aisle, he must give her away, it has been nearly twelve years since his wife died, Ruth is not just a daughter to him, how will he live without her, he feels his heart breaking, with each jarring step down the aisle, his heart fractures, it seems such a long way, will he have any heart left when he gets to the end? He stands to one side and watches the film of his daughter's wedding, it is not real to him, it is the performance of some melodrama and when it is finished, nothing will have changed, he will walk back down the aisle with her, arm in arm, back to the flat in Shoreditch. He doesn't listen to the words that are being spoken, they are unimportant, a piece of dialogue, they mean nothing, what is important is to resume his life with his daughter, the two of them together, it is a good life, there is no need to change any piece of it. He doesn't look at her, in her dress, there is a glow coming from her, but he can't bring himself to look closely, he can't bring himself. He looks instead at his brother Sol, there with his wife, and his brother Danny, with his latest woman friend. He will be alone, he will be without *his* wife all over again, and this time, without Ruth, it will be unbearable. Sol is looking at him, the look is saying: 'pull yourself together, Moishe, pull yourself together.'

At the reception, Ruth introduces herself to Charlie's sister, the only one of his family to be invited. Deborah is perfectly polite, she offers Ruth her congratulations and wishes her every happiness, but she is clearly uncomfortable, if she could she would move away, or leave altogether. Jean comes over, curious to meet Charlie's sister, but Deborah sees this as an opportunity and excuses herself.

Jean is startled but recovers quickly.

"Have I told you how beautiful you look?" she asks Ruth.

"A hundred times."

"Then it must be true."

Ruth is looking at the retreating figure of her sister-in-law.

"Ruthie," Jean says.

"What?"

"It will be fine. Everything will be all right."

THE HOUSE

At first, Charlie and Ruth lived in one of the flats above the shop, third-floor front. 'It won't be for ever,' Charlie promised her but she liked the flat, she liked to stand at the window looking out over the bustle of Wentworth Street. It was only twelve minutes to the office on Commercial Street and twelve minutes back and, after work, she would wait in the shop with him until he closed up and then they would run up the stairs to the flat and make love. Every day, they made love. Then she would cook and they would eat, and then, not always, they would make love again.

"Every day," she tells Jean.

Jean looks worried.

"Every day? You do know, too much sex, it's not good for you."

"What do you mean?"

"I'm joking, Ruthie! I'm jealous. You look fabulous. I have never seen you look so alive."

The brothers see it too. Sol smiles at her. Danny pinches

her cheek. Morris knows that his daughter is truly a woman now, and he holds back from her. He feels embarrassed.

One Saturday, when Ruth is six months pregnant, Charlie says he wants to take her for a drive. She thinks he is taking her to the coast again, but this is the opposite direction.

"Where are we going? Where are you taking me?" she asks.

He won't tell her.

They drive to the edge of London, just before it gives way to farmland. The sun shines and then rests behind clouds before coming out again. He turns into a cul-de-sac and parks in front of a detached house, half-hidden behind a barricade of tall conifers. She wonders who they are visiting, who Charlie knows who could live in such a grand house, and then he takes a set of keys from his pocket and smiles at her.

From the back window of the master bedroom, Ruth looks out, beyond a garden, over fields and trees. She thinks: this is another country, I will be a stranger in a foreign land, I will be an immigrant, I will have to change my ways. In the car, on the way back, she says:

"Charlie, can we afford it? Surely it is too big? Too big a step for us?"

He doesn't look at her.

"Ruthie," he says. "It's not a problem."

She thinks: he has the shop, and he owns the flats, and she thinks that he has been left money when his grandfather died, but even so. What will Jean say? she wonders. She knows what Jean will say: 'what's the matter with you, Ruthie? You're a lucky woman, for heaven's sake, for once in your life, stop worrying.' She wonders whether her father has given him money. She will never ask. She never did understand how Charlie was able to afford a house as big as this house in Stanmore.

They moved in soon after, just before she gave birth. Charlie was determined that they would bring their baby daughter back to their new home. She never told him that she had been happy with what she knew: an apartment, one of several in a building, a community of neighbours, Beth, Judith and Morris a bus ride away. The house is detached, large, with gardens at the front and the back, keeping the world at a distance. The cul-de-sac could be like a community, but it isn't, here everyone is separated, you don't trip over people on the stairs as you climb with the shopping to your apartment on the third floor. Charlie had hated this tumble of lives, other people's noise, the smell of their cooking, the assumed intimacy of neighbourliness. He didn't want to be friendly with these people, to share the stories of their days. He wants to be separate, detached, distinct. He wants to extract himself from his Jewishness. There are no Jewish families in the cul-de-sac. As soon as he gets home, he takes the baby girl in his arms and carries her to his chair in the lounge and she falls asleep on his chest. They call her Irene, after his dead mother.

The house was too big for Ruth. Once the children were at school, she would spend her days in the kitchen, cooking or clearing away or sitting with a coffee at the table where they ate their meals. It was so quiet. When she had finished her coffee and taken the cup to the sink, she would walk into the large hall where the dog was asleep in his basket. She didn't wake him, instead she went into the sitting room that ran the length of the house and walked to the double doors that opened onto the patio at the back. She would look out at the garden. She didn't like the garden, with its lawn and the two big willow trees at the back, lounging menacingly. She never stepped onto the lawn. To her, it was like the sea and she couldn't swim. She didn't want to get wet. She didn't want to drown. She had no interest in gardening. She liked apartments, she liked being above ground. She liked to look down on the world from a safe distance. The house didn't make her happy in the way that it was supposed to. She would leave the sitting room and go back into the hall and into the dining room, and look at her reflection in the surface of the mahogany dining table that was a gift from her father, it seats eight, they never use it, never use the canteen of silver cutlery or the Limoges porcelain, maybe twice a year at most. On the wall is a large framed photograph of Irene, fifteen years old, hair blowing in the wind, she has her father's smile, she is radiant. Ruth goes back to the kitchen, avoiding the study, which also opens off the hall. She hates the study most of all. It has an upright piano which nobody plays, and shelves of books that nobody reads and a roll top desk that no one sits at, and on the desk a studio photograph of the four of them as a family, that nobody looks at. The study sums up the hollow pretension of the house, if she went in, she might give in to her feelings. Instead, she goes back to the kitchen and looks at the recipes in a magazine or leafs through a cookbook. She turns on the wireless and listens to music. She makes a shopping list. She misses her father.

Between the birth of her daughter and the birth of her son, Ruth had two miscarriages. She had thought that she would not be able to have another child, she became unsure that she wanted another child, but this one went to term. Irene, was three years old by then, the apple of Charlie's eye. She would sit on her father's lap when he came back from the shop. Ruth would bring him his gin and tonic and his bowl of salted peanuts and dish of gherkins; she would take off his shoes, untying the laces and lifting them one by one off his feet and replace them with his slippers and all the time Irene would sit in his lap and make him laugh, she would put her head in front of the paper so that he couldn't read it, 'look at *me*', she would say, bright as a button. Ruth would take the shoes through to the kitchen to be cleaned later.

The boy was lifted out of her womb, she felt nothing. Charlie had said he wanted a son, but the baby was not strong. His chest was wrong. His breathing was poor. He was born with no hair, no eyelashes even. He cried. He didn't sleep. They thought he would not live long. The day she came home from the hospital, Charlie brought a dog back with him, a boxer dog, a puppy, she thought it was the ugliest dog in the world. Why a dog? Why *then*? The boy is called David, after her grandfather. He has bad dreams and wakes screaming in the middle of the night. She takes him downstairs so as not to disturb his father, but it is no good. They are all exhausted and Charlie is impatient. He gets angry. She leaves the baby in his pram on the patio in the warm weather and the dog stands guard over him and growls at her when she comes near.

She knew that if she loved David too much, Charlie would be jealous, and that if she didn't love him enough, Charlie would be angry with her. The boy was like a land mine. She was frightened to move. He was a sweet child who bore his infirmities with good grace. His asthma went away. His nightmares stopped. Her happiest time was the few years before he started school, when it was just the two of them in the house. After that, she was left alone with the dog for company. She talked to the dog and the dog listened. It felt good to be listened to. She tells him how she feels: lonely, bored, lost, and the dog seems to understand, would look at her sorrowfully, and then, on a more optimistic note, suggest that they go for a walk because he knows that this often helps to lift her spirits, not always, it is a nice day, she can still talk to him, but maybe the movement and the fresh air and the sights (and for him the smells) will take their minds off their problems, at least for a while. She fetches her shoes and her coat and the lead, the dog tells her she won't need a coat and he won't need the lead. "Just in case," she says. She doesn't much like the outdoors, but she walks the dog down the road and turns right to the gate into the field with trees fringeing a rise in the distance. She lets the dog off the lead and thinks she will wait by the gate and watch him relish the space, but the dog insists on her coming into the field with him, she can stick to the path, but he insists that she must open herself up to this sense of freedom, if only for a short while. She laughs in agreement. The dog thinks that she is beautiful when she laughs.

David spends most of his time in his room. He comes out for meals and sits quietly at the table. He does the washing up when it is his turn. He does what he is told. He is painfully shy. He lacks confidence. Ruth is convinced that he doesn't like her. She knows that he doesn't like Charlie, and thinks that he blames her for Charlie being his father. Or she thinks that he doesn't like her because she didn't love him enough as a baby, though she loves him more now, maybe it is too late, you can never make up for lost time. Or she thinks that he doesn't like her because what is there to like, apart from her cooking? These thoughts confuse and distress her. He squirms away from her when she shows him affection. But then there are times, when she has laid a piece of green baize on the dining room table and lifted the lid on a jigsaw puzzle, he comes and joins her. He sits next to her and sorts through the pieces, finding the edges and passing them on to her so that she can fit them together. And there are times, when she is playing patience at the kitchen table, when he will fetch another pack of cards and will play alongside her. When she can't go any further, she says: "I'm stuffed," and this always makes him chuckle. At those times, she appreciates the quiet companionship that passes between them and she thinks that perhaps he might like her after all.

She looks forward to Charlie coming home in the evening.

He fills the house with his presence. He makes sense of the house, the size of it. His smile can still light up a room and he will take her in his arms and kiss her on the lips and cup her buttocks in his hands and a thrill of electricity flows through her body. She knows he is only playing with her but he still wants her and she still wants him, and she is heartened by this. They don't make love every day now, of course not, with the noise of the children and the reproving look of the dog, but they do still make love and this still animates her, reassures her that she is alive. They lie on their bed in the master bedroom, with the door closed, and she places her head on his chest and he tells her how much he loves her, always has, always will, from the very first time he saw her with that bag of bagels on Wentworth Street.

But there are also days when he fills the house with his bitterness, turns the air dark and thick. She works hard to prepare for his arrival, everything as he likes it, drinks, snacks, the newspaper folded on his armchair in the sitting room. She works hard to prepare herself, to look happy and pleased to see him and grateful for the life he has created for her. She is ready to hug him, to kiss him, to press herself against him, and also ready to hold back and give him space. There is little time for her to decide, and it is best to get it right. She still helps in the shop sometimes. Along with the bulbs and the batteries at the back, he now sells small electricals: kettles and toasters, irons and hairdryers, and he has installed a record counter that sells LPs and EPs and singles, the music that exploded in the sixties. He has put a speaker above the doorway and people come to listen and sometimes to dance. She would work in the shop more often if she could, but he doesn't want her to.

The truth is: Ruth has come to dread Charlie coming home. He is tired when he gets back, she understands this. The journey alone, three hours there and back through London traffic, from Stanmore to Aldgate, it can be a nightmare. And customers can be difficult, or there can be too few of them, or the boy he has working behind the record counter can be annoying, or the music he plays to attract customers can be so irritating, over and over the same stupid songs. But none of this explains the depth of his bitterness, she understands that, she understands that it is his shame, his shame that he has been unable to change this part of his life, that he is still no more than a shopkeeper in a shitty little shop in the Jewish East End, day in day out, and will be for the rest of his life, because he is not smart enough, not brave enough to do anything else. He is not clever like his son because he had never had such an education, had never been given such an opportunity, had never had a father who thought he was any good, who wanted him to do well, who invested in him in the way he has invested in David.

She wants her love for her husband to erase this bitterness, to clear away the dark, thick air. Sometimes she feels that it just might, but when it doesn't, she must not show any sign of her disappointment. She wants him not to be angry, she wants not to be afraid of his anger, she wants her life not to be compressed by his bitterness, she wants there not to be days, at least not so many days, when she shrinks inside of her anxiety as if she were hiding in the cupboard under the stairs. But in spite of all this, she does still love Charlie. He is so handsome, so masculine, so potent. Even when his mood is sour and he barely notices her and finds fault with her efforts to welcome him home, she feels her love for him. She knows that she has to love him. If she doesn't, what then?

One day, Charlie comes home and puts a piece of paper in front of her. She takes it to the kitchen table. It is an official document, it is a certificate, she thinks that someone has died, she is afraid to look more closely. When she does, she sees that the document is the record of a change of name. It shows that he has changed his surname from Podolski to Phillips. She looks at him. She doesn't understand. She looks back at the certificate. Her name is there. So are the children. "We are all called Phillips now," he tells her. He wants her to stop calling him Charlie. From now on it must be Charles. And he will call her Ruth. In the piece of paper that he has placed in front of her, she sees the gap between who he is and who he wants to be. And she sees the gap between who she was and who she is now. She was Ruthie Bernstein and then she was Ruthie Podolski and now she is Ruth Phillips. Who is that? she wonders. Do I know her? Will I like her?

Ruth's father, Morris, comes to see her sometimes, during the day, when Charles is at the shop and the children are at school. Once a month perhaps, not often enough. She makes him lunch, something light, a salad or a sandwich, and they sit at the kitchen table and eat together. She tries hard to hide her unhappiness and he tries hard not to see it, but this house. It should be a source of pride, of pleasure, a sign of arrival, of security, and yet nothing rings true.

In the sitting room, a large copy of Constable's The Hay Wain is hung above the fireplace. Morris studies it: two men in an empty wagon pulled by two black horses across a pond towards some buildings. There is no sign of hay, the water is too shallow and sluggish for a mill. Is it a mill? Where is the wheel? Black clouds are gathering overhead, casting a shadow over the pond and the buildings. The painting makes Morris remember the stetl in Lithuania where he was born, nine years before the turn of the century: there was hay to be carried in wagons just like this from the fields to the barns for the winter, pulled by heavy horses, dogs barking from the banks of streams. Who would have thought then that the man driving the wagon would turn his pitchfork against his Jewish neighbours and take them, in his wagon, to the pits outside Kaunas where they would lie stripped and quivering whilst he reaches for his rifle? Amongst them Morris' mother, his father, his youngest brother, his two sisters, his aunts, his uncles, his cousins. Who knew, when Sol brought his two brothers across Europe to start their lives again in London, who knew then what they had truly left behind? This painting, why is it here, in this house? What does it mean, what truths does it hide? The old bitterness rises in Morris, bile in his throat. He swallows hard.

Morris goes back to the kitchen where Ruth is waiting for him. He knows that she is miserable but then he thinks: there are worse miseries. He blames himself, he blames her, he blames himself. She tells him that his coffee is going cold. "Where do you get your coffee?" he asks her; a shop in the village, they call Stanmore a village apparently. It is good, strong coffee, how much is it? He winces when she tells him. "I'll get you some, next time," she says. He shakes his head.

Ruth tells her father about the change of name. Morris says nothing for a while and she is left wondering what he is thinking.

"Why Phillips?" he asks eventually.

"It is his grandfather's name, Philip Podolski. The sign above the shop?"

Morris remembers the sign. He had not paid it much attention. He thought the shop was small and grubby. He remembers Philip Podolski, there is no pleasure in the memory, he was a sour little man, Polish, calculating.

"Well," he says.

"Well?" she asks.

"Why?" he says.

"What do I know."

"Did he ask you? Did he talk to you?"

She shakes her head.

Morris treads carefully along the line between saying nothing and saying what he thinks. He has never said a word. He knows that it is difficult, that Ruth doesn't tell Charlie - Charles - when her father comes to visit, that Charles doesn't like him and doesn't like the closeness that he shares with his daughter, Morris understands this and takes great pains not to add to his resentment, even if it means that he doesn't see Ruth as much as he would like to and that he doesn't see his grandchildren often either and this is a cause of great sadness to him. He walks from the tube station at the end of the Bakerloo line through the village to the house, twenty minutes at his pace, and, when he turns into the cul-de-sac, he looks around him like a spy, making sure that he is not being watched or followed, making sure that there is no chance that Charles will be there. He is anxious and he tells himself: 'this is ridiculous.' But there you are.

When she had told him last year that David would not have a bar mitzvah, Morris was glad that Sol was not alive to hear this. He said to Ruth: "how will he know he is a man? How will we celebrate his life? How will we give to him?" She could only shake her head. Now he takes the certificate in his hands as if by holding it he might be able to extract some meaning from it. He reads again his daughter's new name. He lays the piece of paper flat on the table.

"Well," he says. "If it makes him happy."

Before he leaves, Morris takes the dog for a walk, down to the fields. He likes the dog. The dog is always pleased to see him, and to see Ruth and her father together. They are at ease with each other and the mood of the house lifts a little when he is there. As they walk, Morris voices his concerns about his daughter, his bemusement with her husband, his frustration with his own powerlessness, and the dog walks alongside him, listening with interest. It is good to know that Morris shares his concerns, and his bemusement, but it is frustrating to hear that he can do nothing to change the situation. The dog wants to shout at him: “do something!” When they reach the field, the dog doesn’t run off as he usually does, he goes with Morris to the bench and he sits beside him and Morris scratches him behind his ears, which the dog absolutely loves.

THE FUNERAL

THEY HAVE GIVEN her medication for the pain in her back, but not for the pain in her heart. The pain in her heart is unbearable. The medication leaves her confused, drifting in and out of awareness. Consciousness is slippery. Ruth knows where she is and then she doesn't. She knows why they have brought her here and then she is not sure. She is in a chair. The chair moves. There is someone behind the chair. They are murmuring to her. They must be pushing the chair. It must be Charlie, Charles, except she knows it isn't, she doesn't know how she knows this, so who is it, who is pushing the chair, who is murmuring to her, she can't make out what they are saying? Whoever it is, they push her past rows of people, seated, they turn to look at her as she glides past, she smiles in acknowledgment, and then drifts away and then focuses again. The chair stops moving, she is at the front of something. The person pushing her sits down next to her, she turns to see who it is, it looks like her son, that cannot be, it cannot be her son, that would not be allowed, she turns away to face forward, where someone is speaking. She hears the name: Morris. Morris Bernstein. This person is talking about her father. Ruth remembers: her father has died. It jars her. The pain in her heart is unbearable. She sobs. The person sat next to her puts their hand on her arm. Where is Charlie? She grips the hand in hers. The pain in her heart. She knows now. She can't breathe. He says to her softly: breathe, breathe. The person speaking stops. Someone else takes their place. She can't listen to what they are saying. Then people stand up. She tries to stand too, pushing against the arms of the chair but the person next to her tells her not to, that it's ok, it's ok. It *is* David, her son, she is sure of it, his voice at any rate, but it can't be. There is a movement, she looks to see what it is, an opening, and then a sliding and a roaring noise, then she understands and she cries out, a long wailing cry, anguished, sobbing, it seems to last forever, people are pierced by it, everyone gathered there at the crematorium, is pierced by the great outpouring of her grief. There seems to be years of feeling in that cry, who knows what feelings, layer upon layer, it is disturbing, will it ever end, and then it does. Ruth is exhausted, she slumps forward in the wheelchair as if all the air has left her body. People look at each other, they breathe again, they would like to move, to shuffle out of the seated rows, but they must wait for her, for the son to push his mother forward towards the garden of remembrance. All this time, Charlie stood between Jean and Izzie, uninterested in Ruth's grief for her father, unable to bring himself to sit next to his son.

In less than two months, the people filing past Ruth now will be back at this same crematorium for her funeral, but today, as is the custom, they must wish her long life. It seems such a cruel thing to do, she is barely alive, but, with tears in their eyes, they take her hand, which is a parcel of bones, that is all, they kiss her hand and they wish her long life. She thanks them graciously, a remembered response. They look up at David, stood behind his mother, and they shake their heads apologetically and then move on and the next person repeats the process. Now it is Jean, with her husband Izzie, and she kneels down and takes her old friend's hands in hers and says: "Oh Ruthie, oh my darling." By the end, Ruth is exhausted, almost asleep in her chair and David wheels her back to the car, where one of the undertakers helps him to lift her onto the back seat. The undertaker folds the wheelchair and puts it into the boot of the car whilst David sits next to his mother and covers her with a blanket. He places a pillow behind her head and settles her back against it and before she does finally fall asleep, she says: 'thank you.' Charles had told his son that he must take care of his mother during the funeral.

Ruth had thought that she would never see him again, her son, which is why, at her father's funeral, she could not believe that it was him behind her wheelchair; Charles would not allow him to be there, to be anywhere near her. He had been so adamant, so angry that she had feared that he might be going mad. This is before she became ill, or rather, it was when she was in remission, when they had thought that she was clear of the cancer, when she was feeling better, getting stronger. She didn't understand how it had happened, but Charles had made it so that she could not see either David or Irene. He had made it so that her children were estranged from her.

Her daughter left home when she was eighteen years old. Before she went, Irene had said to her mother: "I have to get away." Ruth knew that they argued, from the bedroom, she had heard Charlie shouting at Irene and Irene shouting back, Charlie's deep roar of anger, Irene's cries of resistance. Irene determined to have her way, to live her life, to further herself. Charlie refusing to let her, to pour money down the drain. Charlie would not invest in Irene. Ruth did not have the courage to go downstairs to intervene. Her daughter was anyway impatient with her, saw her as weak, as too much under Charlie's thumb. Irene had told her: "I am not going to let him control my life the way he does yours". Ruth had thought: good luck with that, but she had under-estimated her daughter. She heard the front door slam and assumed that Irene would return, but as the days went by, it became clear that she wasn't coming back.

After her daughter had gone, after Ruth had become ill, as she lay resting on her bed, she asked Charlie why Irene felt that she had had to get away. He is sitting at her dressing table, looking at himself in the mirror, he doesn't turn his broad shoulders back to face her. He stays as unmoving and watchful as a heron.

"It's better she's gone," he says, "she'll be back soon enough."

Still he doesn't turn to face her. He has taken the top from a bottle of perfume, is holding it to his nose, it is expensive, a birthday present, is it worth the price? Charlie knows that he hasn't answered Ruth's question with the truth. He never did tell her that Irene had phoned him when news of her mother's illness reached her. He thought that she would beg to come home, or beg for money, or beg for forgiveness. But no. Charlie listened to his daughter as she told him, *told* him, that she was coming back to see her mother. He closed his eyes. He breathed deeply. He tried, he did, to hold back his anger. But *listen to her*: she thought she was so much better than him, her voice, so fucking arrogant. Who did she think she was? He told her to fuck off. He told her she would never see her mother again, over his dead body. He slammed the phone down on her. Ruth never saw Irene again.

Now, after the disastrous phone call with David, when she was in remission, it seemed to Ruth as if Charles had divorced her from both her children. Why would he do that? Did he think that they would upset her? Did he think that he needed to look after her on his own, without their interference? He had always wanted her all to himself. Always. So why did he have children? She didn't understand. She missed her daughter and she missed her son. They were what she had done with her life. Without them, she had done nothing. She sat in the emptiness of their absence, and the cancer, sensing an opportunity, returned.

Back at the house in Stanmore, after her father's funeral, David fetches the wheelchair from the boot and places it by the car and helps his mother into it. Ruth can see that it is her son, that she had been right, that this was not an illusion.

"It is you," she says.

"Yes," he says, "it is alright. He knows I'm here."

"Where is he?"

"He is coming."

Ruth closes her eyes in relief. She had never believed that she would ever see her son again, this is more than she could have hoped for. She wants to look at him but he is behind her, pushing the wheelchair down the path to the front door, they never use the front door. This house.

She remembers the evening clearly; she has replayed it so often in her mind. She would like to think that it had never happened and that David's presence now, after the funeral, was proof that it hadn't. What could she have done differently? She asked her father this one day when he came to the house, before he too became ill. He said that there was nothing that she could have done. Morris could make no sense of it and he was a wise man so what hope was there that she would be able to make sense of it by herself. Charlie's anger seemed to be a force in its own right, disconnected from the present. He had wanted to take her away again, to the coast, sea air. She had suggested that he close the shop for the week, and he had said no, he had said that it was the least he could do, he meant their son, David, the least he could do to manage the shop for them whilst they're away, after all he had done for him, after everything he had done for him. She had said: "but he has already done the shop for us this summer," and he had shouted at her: "well, he can fucking do it again," and when she had tried to reason with him, he had screamed at her: *"you always take his side!"* There was no point talking to Charlie, Charles, when he was like this. And she was still not strong, even though she had been given the all clear, which is why Charlie wanted this extra week, he was doing it for her. Ruth would have been happier staying at home, the thought of packing and the drive and the hotel and the long evenings. They had been away once already that summer and it had exhausted her. But he was determined.

Charlie came to her after the phone call with David and the air turned thick and black. She crumpled inside.

"You are not to speak to that boy again," he said.

She knew to say nothing.

"He put the phone down on me. No-one puts the phone down on me. Least of all him, my own son, after all I have done for him, who does he think he is?"

He turns to Ruth.

"You will not see him, you will not speak to him, you will not write to him, do you understand me?"

She nodded.

"Bastard!" he shouts. "Selfish little bastard!"

She closed her eyes.

"He is dead to me," he said.

Ruth never asked Charles what transpired on that phone call. She thought his anger would subside but it did not. She has never fully understood his anger and resentment towards the boy but she sees that it has now crystallised, that it is now hardened and insoluble. His face is defiant, tight lipped, smouldering, his rock face. He sits in his chair in the sitting room brooding, the paper unread in his lap.

What is she supposed to do? She is still recovering, she is not strong, her life is with this man. She loves him and she does not doubt that he loves her. When she says to him: "Charles, would you mind if we didn't go away? I'm so tired. I think it would be better for me just to rest, here, would you mind?", he agrees immediately, to her surprise, she thought he might force her to go, to insist that it would be better for her, but he agreed that they could spend the time together here, at the house. And then he opened the shop that week, went in every day. Ruth thought: this is madness.

One day, when Morris is ill, he wakes in his room in the Masonic Hospital. He has his own room, not big, a bed, chairs, bland pastel pictures on the wall, to his left, machines flashing and beeping, a drip on a stand, God knows what they are putting in to him, he wishes they would stop. He sees his grandson, David, sitting in a chair by the window, looking out at the view. He has a room with a view, even though from the bed all he can see is the tops of some trees. Sol would tell him to count his blessings.

Morris thinks: 'he has come all this way to see me.'

David looks up, he is a young man now, and smiles at his grandfather.

"You shouldn't have come," says Morris, "all this way."

"You asked me to. You wanted to see me."

"Did I? Why?" Morris is confused.

David brings the chair back to the bedside. He laughs.

"I don't know. It doesn't matter. I'm here."

"It does matter." Morris knows that it matters but he can't for the life of him remember why.

His grandson brings him some water. "It's ok. It will come back to you."

Morris drinks the water.

"How is your mother?" he asks, and then he remembers. "Have you spoken to her?"

"I phone her when I can," David tells him.

"How is she?"

"Not good."

"No."

Morris drinks some more water. His throat is dry. He also is not good. The water makes him cough, which hurts and which is exhausting. When he has his breath back, Morris says:

"I need you to do something for me."

"What?" The boy is instantly suspicious.

Morris points a shaking finger at him: "you can't refuse the wishes of a dying man."

David looks so much like his father, he is stubborn. Charles would have no hesitation in refusing the wishes of a dying man, would probably take pleasure in it, is his son the same, surely not? David refills the glass with water and places it on the table beside the bed.

"So tell me, what is your dying wish?" asks this young man, his grandson, smiling.

"Speak to him," Morris says firmly.

David recoils. "No."

Morris closes his eyes in despair.

"You must. For your mother's sake," he insists.

David walks over to the window, he is angry.

"Why should it be me?" he says.

"It can only be you."

"He'll say no."

"You will have tried. That is all I ask."

"It will make things worse. For her."

Morris thinks: 'can things be worse?'

He waits a moment. “Well?” he asks.

David comes back to the bed and kisses his grandfather’s hand.

“I will do this for you. I will do it for her.”

Morris sighs with relief.

“You’re a good boy,” he says.

Charles stares at the letter that his son has written. He looks at the handwriting, lower case. He had never learnt to write in lower case, he writes in block capitals, not that he writes much, laborious, ugly marks on paper. The boy writes well, the writing and the words and their meaning. The letter splits him in two. At the same time, he feels both fury and he feels panic. Is this how it has been all my life, he wonders, fury and panic? His wife is dying, he is doing everything he can, he will fight this with everything in his power, he refuses to let her die. He is not ready for her to die. This is the woman who, the first time he saw her, outside the shop, he knew that she was the woman he will marry. He has held her close to him from that moment. Nothing else matters. And still she wastes away before his eyes. Still she refuses to get well. And this boy, with his fancy handwriting and his education, who dared, in spite of everything, dared to put the phone down on me, to say *no* to me, after all I have done for you, you will do what I say, this is not a discussion, you don’t get to fucking reason with me, I don’t give a fuck about your plans! Your plans! This is your mother I am doing this for, your mother, a holiday for your sick mother, sea air, for her. Don’t you put the phone down on me, don’t you dare put the phone down on me, you little shit, you little fucking shit, you selfish little fucking shit, you piece of shit. And now he writes, in this letter: ‘for my mother’s sake’. He dares to say it. Now!

Charles wants to tear up the letter. Fuck him. But he

doesn't. He wants to scream. All his life he has fought against people who wish him harm and he has beaten them, every time, every one, he has punished them, banished them, cut them out, disowned them, disinherited them, set fire to his memories of them, there have been so many of them, so many people who have wished him harm. He had never once wavered, never once, once his mind is made up, that is it, there is no turning back. No weakness. They are dead to him. This letter, he doesn't know how, doesn't know why, but it has got to him. He is so alone. Ruth is leaving him, he is holding on to her, but she is slipping away and he thinks of her, he knows what it would mean to her to see her son again, to see him before she dies. He can't deny her that, not now, not so near the end. He has asked too much of her, he sees that, the price was too high. He is sat at the desk in the study, the photograph of the four of them, the family, by his elbow, and he is split in two. He puts his head in his hands.

He writes, in block capitals: YOU CAN COME. YOU CAN SEE HER. YOU CAN STAY. FOR YOUR MOTHER'S SAKE. He doesn't sign it. He writes it on a piece of card, puts the card in an envelope, addresses the envelope. It takes him three days to post it.

PART III

END OF LIFE CARE

MORRIS

THE DOOR OPENS and he can smell her before he sees her. Perfume and cigarettes. Not so cheap these days, the perfume. Time was he could tell you which one, now his sense of smell is leaving him, all his senses are edging away from him. They don't want to be associated with a dying man.

"Hello Jean," Morris says, and he opens his eyes and there she is, a ball of fur and makeup and hair and warmth.

"Moishe," she says. She stands by his bed and smiles at him for a moment.

He can tell she is shocked by the sight of him, the tubes and wires, the bags of fluid hovering in mid-air, the machines, the flashing lights, his old body, readying itself.

"You look terrible," Jean chuckles, her wheezing cackle of a laugh.

"And you look a million dollars." It's true, she does.

She leans over and kisses Morris on both cheeks.

"I've brought these for you," a box of chocolates, "expensive," she says, "Izzie sent them. He wanted to send you some rollmop, I told him: 'Izzie, for God's sake, he's in hospital.'"

She puts them on the table beside the bed.

"If you don't want them, don't worry, I'll have them."

"Tell him thank you, tell him they're my favourite."

She smiles with satisfaction.

"Have one," Morris tells her.

"I couldn't."

He knows that not to be true.

She wriggles out of her fur coat and pulls up a chair and takes hold of his free hand, the one with no tubes, no bruises.

"So how is Izzie?" Morris asks.

Jean rolls her eyes.

"How would I know? He's so busy, Mo, I never see him. We are ships in the night."

"He has done well."

"He never forgets what you did for him."

"Izzie was the best investment I ever made."

"Sandwiches, Mo. Who knew?"

"Who knew? Izzie knew. He saw the future."

"People are in such a hurry now. They don't stop for lunch. They eat at their desks, they eat while they walk, in the street, on the bus. The world has gone mad."

"It's good for business."

"That's what Izzie says."

"What about the railway stations?"

"They're talking, that's all he tells me, they're negotiating, and the service stations on the motorways. It doesn't make him happy, Mo, all the time he frets, he worries, he doesn't sleep, just like Sol, remember?"

Does he remember Sol? Could he ever forget Sol? Sol, the eldest, first and foremost, the one who brought them over, the one who brought them up, like a father. Sol, who had left behind so much more than they did. Morris close his eyes, and there he is, his brother Sol, old before his time, saying the Kaddish every Friday for all those that we lost.

"He never recovered, Jean. It hit him hard, hardest of all, he never recovered. Some didn't. Sol didn't."

"Izzie's parents the same."

What can he say? Morris closes his eyes.

"He says: 'if only my father could see me now,'" Jean says. "What do I say to him, Mo, what can I do?"

"Tell him: '*I* see him.' Tell him: '*I'm* proud of him.' Tell him: 'he is like a son to me.'"

He hears her crying softly as she squeezes his hand.

"You were lucky," he tells her.

"I know that."

"To be able to sit with your father. To be with him at the end. Like you're sitting with me now."

She is looking at her face in a small mirror, dabbing at the tears with a tissue.

She says firmly: "she would come if she could, Mo. You know that."

He knows that this is true. He knows that Ruth would visit him if she could, that it would be her, not Jean, sitting there now by his bedside, that this is what he wants more than anything. He loves Jean, he does, but he so wants her to be Ruth.

"How is she?" he asks.

"I had to tell her: 'Ruthie, you can't go, you're not strong enough, don't ask him, don't say anything.'"

Don't ask him. Charlie. Morris can't bear it. He closes his eyes. He doesn't want to hear this. He wants to die.

He looks into her eyes. "Unplug me, Jeanie, please."

She is startled. She looks around the room to find which plug he's talking about and for a second, he thinks she might do it. If anyone could do it, it would be Jean.

"I can't, Mo. I can't do it, you know that, don't you? If I could, I would, I promise."

"I have to die before Ruth does, Jean. I couldn't bear it."

Jean takes his hand again.

"She feels the same."

Morris closes his eyes and sets his head back against the pillow.

Jean tries to change the subject, to lighten the mood.

"So, tell me, what is the food like in here?" She sniffs as if she might be able to smell a trace of his last meal. Morris is not interested in the food.

"Do you hear anything of David?" he asks her.

Jean gets up from the chair and walks over to the window. In the grounds, there is one of those dogs, a bull terrier, horrible, cocking its leg against a tree. Jean frowns, but the owner is a woman, nice looking in a not cheap coat, smoking a cigarette.

Jean has never forgiven David for abandoning Ruth. Irene too. These children: who do they think they are? She is under no illusions about Charlie, but whatever happened, to abandon your mother like that, it is unnatural. As far as Jean is concerned, it is the children who have made Ruth sick, the misery they caused her, she can't forgive them. The boy especially, his own mother. She has boys, they would do anything for her. And Mo asks if she has heard anything of *David*!

"He came to see me," Mo tells her.

Jean wheels round to look at him. "When?"

What does it matter when? How am I supposed to know when? Morris thinks, the days here bleed into one another, they aren't days any more.

"I don't know when."

"Why?"

Jean, these questions, they don't help, they're not the right questions, let me tell this in my own way.

"I asked him to. He's not a bad boy, Jean. He's a good boy."

Jean stares at the old man, so frail inside the white envelope of his hospital bed. How can he think this? She cannot believe that this is what Morris thinks.

She comes back to the chair and sits down. She opens the box of chocolates and takes one.

"You want?" she holds out the box to him.

The last thing he wants. He shakes his head.

"How did he know where you are?" she asks.

"He phones his mother."

Morris can see that Jean is not sure whether to trust what he is saying.

"It's true, Jean."

"It is the least he can do," she says grudgingly.

Morris doesn't understand why Jean is so angry.

"He abandoned her, Mo," she says. "His mother is dying, he does nothing."

"It is Charlie, Jean, he won't let the children come home, he won't let Ruth talk to the children. It is Charlie, he has cut them off from her."

Jean shakes her head loose from these words. Charlie had told her that the boy wanted nothing more to do with them. Irene too, the children had turned their back on their own family. Ruth tells her, even now, how upset Charlie was, how angry, after all he had done for them, how she is worried that Charlie is losing his mind. Jean knows Charlie is difficult, that he was hard on the boy, but this ingratitude, there is no excuse for that. It's about the bond between mother and son; you don't break that bond. How Ruth looked after the boy, how she nursed him, and this is all the thanks she gets.

Morris is desperate.

"I need you to do something for me, Jean."

"Anything. You know that."

"I need you to speak to Charlie."

She takes another chocolate.

Jean had stopped asking them whether they had heard from

the children: Charlie's face, like stone, 'like the whole of him had turned to stone,' Izzie said. Ruth looking at the floor. It can't be easy for Ruthie, she can see that, but Charlie loved her, and in the end, that is all that matters: he loved her. Jean goes back to the window to look out at the view. The woman and the dog have gone.

Morris raises his weak voice to make sure that she can hear.

"I told David to write to Charlie. I told him to ask his father to let him be with his mother before she died, to let him come home. For his mother's sake." Morris is finding this so tiring. "Jean, tell Charlie, for Ruth's sake, tell him: 'read the letter'."

Ruth would never say a word against Charlie, but Jean knows there were issues. There was something not right about him, behind all the charm: the falling out with his father, the problems with the grandfather, what a family! Charlie was no innocent, she knows that, she knows that he had turned his grandfather against his father, and then that he had turned against both of them, so maybe, she thinks now, in this bare hospital room, maybe he got what he deserved. What goes around comes around. But not Ruth, poor sweet Ruthie, she did nobody any harm.

Morris can't help it, he starts to cry. Jean comes over to him and as best she can she puts her arm round him.

"Oh Mo," she says, "my darling. Of course I'll speak to him."

He doesn't stop crying, she holds on to him, she starts crying too.

"Mo," Jean says, "you can't blame yourself. You weren't to know. Who's to know how people will turn out. Look at Izzie. I didn't know he would become a sandwich magnate. He sold rollmop and chopped liver on Wentworth Street. I didn't know he would be a neurotic, who's neurotic when they are young? We are not psychic, none of us, not even you. The future keeps its secrets from us, Mo, you know this."

"There were signs."

"Signs, that's all they were."

"You liked Charlie," he is accusing her.

"Yes, I liked Charlie," she admits.

"She loved him," Morris says in his defence.

"She still does."

"Does she?"

"She still loves Charlie, Mo, and he loves her. In his own way."

She hands him a tissue and he blows his nose.

"Even so," Morris says.

"Even so what?"

"Look at her now."

"You can't blame him for that. Mo, you can't. That's not fair."

She drops the tissue into the waste bin.

But I do, Jean. Morris thinks this, he doesn't say it. But I do. I blame him for everything, for his anger, for his stubbornness, for his foolish pride, for all the misery he has caused, for the fact that my daughter is lying on her deathbed at the same time as I am lying on mine. And I blame myself. I knew. I knew then. I could see. And still I let her marry him. This is how he tortures himself in the days that are left to him.

Jean looks at her watch. It is time for her to go.

"I'll speak to him, Mo. Don't worry," she says.

"He listens to you."

He can tell by her face that this might not be true, and in truth, he knows it not to be true. She shakes her head again.

"He doesn't listen to anyone, Mo, not at the moment."

Not ever, thinks Morris. When did Charlie ever listen to anyone?

"Try."

"I promise."

"Mo, before I go," Jean, with her coat in her hand, "and

I'm sorry to ask, Izzie asked me to ask you this. It's your shares in the company. I told him, it's none of our business, he said 'it *is* my business, that's exactly what it is.'"

"He is right. It is his business."

"He's thinking, if it helps you, he would buy them from you. For a good price, Mo, of course."

Morris' poker face.

"Or at least, if not, then at least, to know your plans, Mo, what you plan to do with them. I told him it's wrong to think of this now. He thinks you won't leave them to Ruth, so will you leave them to Charlie? That's what he is worried about."

Morris shuts his eyes.

"Tell him: I won't leave them to Charlie."

She sighs with relief.

"So ..." she starts the next question.

He stops her: "I'm leaving them to David, Jean."

Jean looks at Morris. This is not what she expected. She nods her head slowly, weighing the information, watching the scales tilt this way and that.

"Have you told him?" she asks.

"No."

"Will he want them?"

"I don't know."

"Will he know what they mean? Will he know what to do with them?"

"I don't know."

She laughs suddenly.

"We'll have to sit down with him."

Morris smiles.

"Make him a sandwich."

"You are a clever bugger, Mo Bernstein. Sol was smart, but you are smarter."

"He's a good boy, Jean. Forgive him. Forgive him for leaving. If not for me, for Ruth."

She wriggles back into her coat and this reminds her of something else, the other question that she came with and wants answering before it is too late.

"Do you remember your camel hair coat, Mo?"

"What about my camel hair coat?"

"Ruthie told me you told her it was made from the hair of the camel you rode in the camel corps?"

His poker face again.

"Were you really in the camel corps, Mo?"

"It was the Imperial Camel Corps."

Jean gasps: "I don't believe you."

She laughs her wheezing cackle of a laugh.

"Who knew, Mo," she says. "What lives we have lived."

"I have left the coat to Izzie," he tells her, smiling, he is teasing her.

"No!" she says. "It's too big, it'll kill him, he'll drown in it."

The thought of little Izzie in that coat, Morris laughs in spite of himself.

She hugs him, holds him tightly for a moment, pulls back, kisses him on both cheeks.

"Goodbye, Mo," she says.

Before she leaves, she takes one more chocolate.

"These are good," she says.

"Take them," Morris tells her, and she does.

CHARLIE

I DIED OF A STROKE. Complications arising. I lay on the floor in the flat, near the door, for five hours. I thought I would die there but they found me. Took me to hospital. I lay in this bed in a ward full of people. The noise. I tried to tell them: 'I have insurance.' I tried to tell them: 'I want to go private,' but I couldn't speak, I opened my mouth, nothing came out. They took good care of me, I'll say that. But all those premiums for nothing.

You know what did it? I had a row with my daughter. Irene. She called me. Out of the blue. I hadn't heard from her in forty years. The things she said. I was upset. She was angry. Angry with me, "I'm an old man, for God's sake," I told her, "it's ancient history." On and on she goes. Who does she think she is? I'm not putting up with this. I put the phone down on her. I take a breath, I think: I need to lie down, and I walk towards the bedroom and then this great bang in my head and I'm on the floor and I can't move.

Do you know what she said? It was stupid. She was crazy. Wild. Like an animal, screaming at me. Of course I was upset, who wouldn't be. She said that I was to blame for everything. For David, for Ruth, for Ruth's death, for Christ's sake! She said that I had damaged *her*, her mental health. Mental health! What the fuck is mental health?

I tried to say to her: "after all these years, Irene. After all these years." I told you she was crazy. I couldn't stop her, on and on, about Ruth, about she died because of me. Nothing could be further from the truth. I did everything I could to keep her alive. I insisted, that last blood transfusion, the doctors said no, Ruth said no, I insisted, if there's a chance, however small. The thing is, and I've never said this before, I think Ruth *wanted* to die. No, wait, wait a minute, that's not right. I think she no longer wanted to live. There's a difference. What do you think that was like for me? How would you feel? I hated her, that bit of her.

What about her mental health, my daughter? I loved that girl. I treated her like a princess. She had everything she ever wanted. So how does she make out that it's my fault that she's unhappy. I tried to ask her: "you're unhappy? Why are you unhappy?" She was crying down the phone. "I don't need this," I told her. "What do you expect me to do about it? You're on the other side of the world. What do you want from me?" She was always too clever for her own good, Irene, always thought she was smarter than me. She wanted to go to university. I told her: "know your place, girl!" I told her: "if you think I am going to waste my money on university." Who did she think she was? I told her: "you can go to college, learn to type, like your mother." What does she think I am, made of money?

Mental health. When did that happen? You just got on with your life. You don't think too much. You block things out. Her generation had it easy and they make out that no-one ever had it so hard and it's all my fault. You want to know hard? You want to know what I did in the war? I'll tell you, and I *did* have it easy, I know that. You know what I was: groundcrew. You know what I did: I loaded bombs onto Lancasters.

I was eighteen. I worked under the armourer. We winched the bombs into the fuselage, at the front of the plane, under the pilot. 1000lb bombs, and incendiaries in a small bomb container. It was hard work. We did Hamburg. We did Dresden. It was our job. You don't think: what am I doing? you just do it, and you think: they deserve it. Look what they did to London, I saw what they did to London, Ruthie's mum died in the bombing, a lot of people died, but then you think, afterwards, you take a minute, you think about what you have done and you think: shit. And then you stop there, you stop thinking. What good does it do?

Once, once, I painted a star of David on a thousand pounder. I thought: fuck them, the bastards, the Germans, obviously. The armourer saw it. After that, they called me 'the Yid'. They called me 'Jewboy'. I thought: fuck this. I didn't do it again.

My son came to see me. David. I think it was him. I don't know. They say, when you're dying, you see things; they say your life flashes before you. I don't know what's real anymore. He stood by my bed and looked down at me. No affection. I don't know which one of them hated me more, my son, my daughter. I tried to speak to him but it would have been just sounds to him, noises, like an animal. You know what I tried to say: 'get me out of here'. How did he find out where I was? They must have contacted him. I'm surprised he came. Maybe he didn't. Maybe it was a dream, I don't care, real or not, I'm pleased he's there, I am, he came to see me, my son, David, after all these years, after everything. I am crying, he takes a tissue and wipes my face for me.

That phone call. That summer. About the shop. He put the phone down on me, you know that? You don't do that, not to me, you don't. That was it. David now, at the end of the bed, he's saying: 'I said I'd come.' I'm thinking: fuck you. He's saying: 'I said I'd come Tuesday.' I tell him: 'you come Monday. You don't come Monday, you're dead to me, you hear me, you'll never see me again, you'll never see your mother again, I'll cut you off, you'll get nothing.' He tries to reason with me - don't you fucking reason with me - he says: 'I'll come Tuesday. What difference does a day make? I'm already changing my plans for you.' His fucking plans. He puts the phone down on me. *He* puts the phone down on *me*. I'm standing there, he cuts me off, nobody cuts me off. Nobody. That's it. He's dead. He's dead to me.

He's still there, standing at the end of the bed, arrogant little shit, and he's telling me what I said, as if I don't know what I said. I tell him: 'whatever I said, it's your fault.' I tell him: 'who are you to tell me what to do, when to open, when to close, who the fuck do you think you are, telling me when you will come. Changing your plans for me!' I didn't give a fuck about his plans. 'I don't give a fuck about your plans.' I might have thought it. I never said it. He says I said it, he says: 'that's why, that's why I put the phone down.' He says: 'because that's the truth, isn't it, you didn't give a fuck about my plans. You didn't give a fuck about me. You don't give a fuck about anyone.' 'This is for your mother,' I scream at him, 'this is for your mother. Your mother, you little shit, it's for her, you can't do this for your own mother?' He shrugs, cocky little bastard. He shakes his head. He turns his back on me. He can fuck off. Who does he think he is? 'You're dead to me' I shout after him, except I don't, because I can't.

Thing is: he's right: I don't give a fuck about anyone. Who does? Who does? In the end, that's it, isn't it? All that matters, *all* that matters is *you*. One life. I don't know. Who knows? All my life, I put myself first, you've got to, no-one else is going to do it, no-one else did do it. You love people, they hurt you. That's the truth. Even Ruthie, and she loved me Ruthie, I know that, bless her, but in the end, she left me. He's right, David: never give a fuck about anyone else.

A nurse comes and gives me a bed bath. She is rough, I must be heavy, a dead weight, I try to help but nothing happens, so she is pulling and pushing, I want to say to her: why are you bothering, but no words. What is the point of thoughts if you can't speak? She washes my genitals, for God's sake, and I'm thinking no erection please, that would be embarrassing, but nothing, as far as I know, she is gentle actually, I like her, nice face, she is being kind to me. She talks to me like she knows I understand her.

Deborah came to see me, standing at the end of the bed. My sister. She is so old now. Is she dead or alive? I'm not sure. This can't be real. This *is* a dream. The thing about Deborah, I remember when we went to get her. We're in a cab, my mother, father, me, and we get to this house, and the cabbie is told to wait, and we go in and my mother takes me to this woman and this girl and she points to the woman and says: 'this is my sister' and she points at the girl and says: 'this is *your* sister. This is your auntie Pat and this is Deborah, your sister, and she is coming home with us, she is coming to live with us now.' I can hear voices, the two men arguing, my father and Deborah's father, except it wasn't Deborah's father, was it? That's the point. I am five years old. Deborah is three years older. I had no idea. Never.

Deborah had no idea either, in the cab on the way back, she is crying, she is saying 'I want my mummy', and my mother is saying: '*I'm* your mummy,' and Deborah is going 'no you're not', and she is sobbing and my mother gets angry with her and my father is holding her back and I'm thinking: 'why have you done this to me, you're my mother, we were happy, the two of us, why have you done this to me?' This is misery. Deborah crying, my mother angry with her, my father angry with my mother and me backing into the corner, as far away from this as possible, I don't want to be here. This is misery. My life was never the same.

A doctor is shining a light in my eyes: what's he looking for? he won't find it. I won't let him. I try to shut my eyes. I can't. He's asking me questions. Is he taking the piss? He's a doctor. What does he want: a conversation?

Ruthie was the light of my life. I wouldn't do anything to hurt her. Surely everyone knew that, anybody could see that. It was just – my mother died when she was fifty-two and Ruth died when *she* was fifty-two. That's not right, is it? Talk about history repeating itself. That's too much. That's not fair. I couldn't handle it. I knew she was dying, of course I did. I just didn't want her to. That's all I asked. She couldn't do that for me. After all I did for her.

When I was courting Ruth, Morris came to the shop to see me. I didn't like Morris. Smug, I thought, the three brothers, thought they were better than the rest of us. They were the same, just smarter, that's all. I could tell he didn't like me. I wasn't good enough for his Ruthie. Fuck him.

Morris looked around the shop. He had never been inside before. He pointed to one of the chandeliers.

"Does your father still make these?"

My father. Don't you talk to me about my father. Don't you come in here and ask about my father. I know what you're doing.

I lie to him: "he's retired."

"But the workshop? Is it still going?"

I know that Morris wants to ask about the ownership of the workshop, who did my grandfather leave it to and why he didn't leave it to my father, and why he didn't leave it me either, his only grandson. But I'm not going to tell him because it's none of his fucking business, and what would he think if I told him? Nothing good of me, that's for sure. Nothing good of his precious daughter's future husband.

"It's still going," that's all I tell him. I dare him: go on, ask me another.

"I brought you a bagel," he says, "lox, no capers. Is that right?"

Clever. I'll give him that. I took his bagel.

We struck a deal that day, Mo and me, and we both came away thinking less of the other. I thought less of him for giving me the money and he thought less of me for taking it. I thought: if you want your daughter living in a big house, Morris Bernstein, I'll make sure it's as far away from you as possible. There he is, at the end of the bed now, that can't be right, he's dead, I'm seeing things, God help me, I'm seeing ghosts, but just in case, I tell him:

'I didn't need your money, Mo. I took it, but I didn't need it.'

The noise in this place. It's bedlam. This is *exactly* what I didn't want. I wanted a room of my own. Separate. Detached. Quiet. Pretty nurses coming in and out. Good doctors, I don't care if they're not English, just that they are polite, respectful, know what they are doing. Decent food, not that I'm eating anything. When it comes down to it, what does it matter: you're dying, you're dead. Except that it was what I worked for, all those years. Is it too much to ask?

Where's Ruthie? Why hasn't she come to see me? Shouldn't she be here? I've seen every bugger else. Is she angry with me? Ruthie, I'm sorry. I didn't mean to hurt you. Is that what I did? Is Irene right, our daughter, is that what I did, I cut you off from them, your children, I made you miserable? I made you ill? Did I? You don't make someone ill, not like that, that's not how it works. I loved that woman. Love doesn't make you ill. That last transfusion, Ruthie, I'm sorry, that was bad, that was wrong. For that I'm sorry. Someone wipes the tears from my face.

Memories are like bombs. Mine are anyway, incendiary

devices packed into a small bomb container under the cockpit. I'm like the plane, that big fucking plane, full of bombs, better not drop them, don't let them go, the damage they could do. I flew round and round with those memories inside of me, I still am, holding on to them, holding on to them for dear life.

My mother comes to see me. This is a nightmare, I don't want this, I tell her to go away. She died when I was twenty-one. She went crazy, after the war, when news of the camps came out, when you found out who lived, who died, she went crazy, it was impossible, my father couldn't cope, he disappeared inside himself. I hated him for it, leaving me to manage everything, the only sane one among them. I'll tell you: it was a relief when my mother died, she was a hard woman, cold, no heart. She is cold now, at the end of the bed, looking down at me. I ask her: 'why? Why did you go and get her? Nothing was the same, poor Deborah, you broke her. Why would you do that to her?' She won't answer, she won't speak, she looks down at me, 'what?' I shout at her, '*what*?'.

I died in that bed, in that ward. Pneumonia, like my mother. I never did get out. They took good care of me, I'll say that for them, and I'm grateful. Thank you. At the end, Ruthie did come, stood close by me. She came with Irene and David, I don't think I ever saw the three of them together like that, Ruth in the middle, her arms around her children, holding them close. I thought: three against one. I thought: I'm on the outside, again. It's exactly what I didn't want. *Exactly* what I didn't want. But I was pleased for her, I was. Pleased for all of them. It is how it should be, I know that. I'm pleased for them.

They stood there, the three of them, looking down at me. I wanted Ruthie to say something, but she didn't. I thought: are they laughing at me, lying here, fucking useless? They weren't. I don't know what they were doing, what they were thinking, glad to see the back of me probably, who can blame them? No love lost, that's for sure. 'I don't want your pity,' that's what I wanted to say to them. I don't think they were offering me pity.

I look back at my life: no regrets. I made it. I made it out and I made it up and ok I was stuck in the shop, I know that, I should have done more, but still, look at my life, the house, Ruth, and after Ruth, the lifestyle, I had money, I lived a full life, I travelled, good food, good wine, friends, women. I wanted for nothing. How many people can say that? I had fun. Fun. Morris Bernstein never had fun, I'll tell you that, not one day of his life. *I* had fun.

You know what I really wanted to say to the three of them, standing by the side of my bed, looking down at me, looking down their noses at me? What I wanted to say to all of them? 'My life has been a success', that's what, 'I don't care what anybody says.' I wanted to shout it, in big letters, big block letters: 'MY LIFE HAS BEEN A SUCCESS!'

DAVID

After all this, Ruth thinks. She has finished reading the book that David wrote for her, *An Imagined Life.* She pushes it away and closes her eyes and sighs and sits back in her chair and looks in on herself. To see yourself as others see you, as they imagine you, she is not sure what she thinks, even less sure what she feels. A shoal of memories swirl at the bottom of the river of her life, muddying the water. She is unsettled.

She decides that she wants to see her son again. This time, she does not wait for an invitation; perhaps David is avoiding her, perhaps he thinks she will be angry with him. Is she angry with him? Is this why she wants to see him: to tell him off? How dare he? How dare he tell her story? She *is* angry. And yet: *is* it her story? It is a story, built from fragments, as if he had taken a few stones from the bottom of her river and what? laid them out in a particular order, added something to them, some powder, and conjured up an imagined life.

When Ruth arrives, David is in bed. The bed is in the living room. He does not look well. He is thin and pale. Is it serious? It looks serious. She sits with him for a while in silence. He might be asleep, but he might be lying there with his eyes shut, avoiding her. She thinks that probably her son had not wanted her to come and is waiting for her to go away. He wakes up and is surprised to see her. He realises that she has come to visit him, again. He wasn't expecting her.

"I am so pleased that you came," he says.

"Are you sure?"

David smiles at her.

"I am glad you didn't wait for an invitation."

"Why did you do this?" She is holding the book. "It's not me."

"Is this you?" he asks. "Here, now?"

She has to think about this.

"If it isn't me, who is it?" she asks.

"A version of you?"

"I have versions?"

"We all have versions."

"Is that a good thing?"

It hurts him when he laughs, it turns into a hacking cough.

She makes him a cup of weak tea. He insists on getting up and sits in his dressing gown and slippers at the kitchen table. He was always a sickly child. Always something wrong with him.

"Who would want to read that stuff?" Ruth asks.

"I wrote it for you. For your eyes only."

She is pleased. She doesn't want anyone else to read it. It can sit there, safe, between the two of them. She is touched that he would go to so much trouble, just for her.

"Drink your tea," she says, pointing at the mug she has placed in front of him. She is not used to mugs like this. It is made not bought, little blue flowers hand-painted on a pale background. She wonders: did his wife make it?

David doesn't drink the tea; he is lost in thought. Ruth watches her son. She remembers how illness turns you in on yourself. She doesn't want to upset him. She doesn't want to argue with him. She is not sure why she has come, she didn't know he was so ill, she is not sure what it is that she wants from this second visit. She looks for something positive to say.

"I like me now more than me then." She doesn't know this until she says it.

David turns his attention back to her.

"Why is that?" he asks.

"I have a sense of humour."

"Yes."

"I'm cleverer."

"Yes."

She can see that he is pleased. She realises something.

"This is who you wanted me to be," she says.

David takes her hand.

"This is how I imagine you now," he says. "That is all."

Ruth looks at him. What does he mean?

"Surely I wasn't that unhappy?" she asks. "Was I?"

"I hope not," he says, and she believes him.

He is tired and says he needs to lie down and he goes back to bed. She stays in the kitchen and clears away the cups and looks out of the window at the view. It *is* a lovely view. She remembers the walk that they went on during her first visit, how unwilling she had been, how she had complained. She smiles with pleasure when she thinks about the block of limestone that his kids used to climb. She would give anything for him to be able to take her on that walk now, she would not complain, she would enjoy his appreciation of the fields and trees and sheep, she would be prepared to learn for herself how to appreciate the beauty laid before her. It is such a shame:

whatever little you learn in life you learn too late. She walks across to the door to the garden and says to the view: 'teach me'.

Ruth watches from a distance as various people come and go. A nurse, who is kind to him, taking his pulse and his blood pressure and his temperature, asking him to rank the pain he is feeling on a scale of one to ten. She writes notes and leaves him some medication and explains what is likely to happen next. A cleaner, who flirts with him as she wipes the surfaces, (just moving the dust around, thinks Ruth); he perks up when the cleaner is there, she makes him laugh. His son, Simon, who brings him a newspaper and tells him how his work is going, a string of words that mean less than nothing to Ruth but David seems to understand, asking questions and giving encouragement. His granddaughter, Jess, hiding her distress behind a screen of bossiness, telling him what he should be doing and what to drink and what to eat, which he receives with good grace. A friend, whom he helps to finish a crossword, so clever, her son, even now. Or maybe the friend is pretending that they need help. But still, he helps them.

"Where did you get your cleverness from?" Ruth asks her son when they are alone again.

David closes his eyes. Ruth thinks he is too tired and wants to sleep, but he asks her:

"Do you remember our dentist?"

She does actually. A cavernous Jew with a heavy beard and a gravelled voice.

"He used to scare me," she says. She remembers his name: "Doctor Maybaum."

"Yes! When I told him I was going to university, he said: 'well, there's a triumph of environment over genetics.'"

She has to think about this for a moment.

"What did you say?"

"He was poking around in my mouth at the time."

It had been one of the few times when he had caught a glimpse of what someone else thought about his parents.

"He was so proud of you," she said. "University. Your father."

"I would never have known."

"Of course not."

"It was just something else he bought with his money. Like the house. Or the car."

"He wanted the best for you."

David looks at her.

"I'm not sure it was ever about me. Or you."

She looks away.

"Maybe you're right," she says.

Ruth boils a chicken, just like the old days, for Morris and her uncles — Charlie had never liked boiled chicken — and made a broth for David, with noodles and carrot and even some chopped egg, and brings it to him in bed. He sits up, the rain is lashing against the windows. Just the smell of the broth revives him, he looks at her with gratitude and brings the spoon to his lips.

"It will be hot," she warns him. He blows on the spoon.

David says to her, out of the blue:

"Tell me about your mother."

Ruth looks at him. What is this? Why is he asking this? This is the last time I make him chicken soup if this is what it does to him.

"She died when I was thirteen," she says.

"I know," he says.

"She sent me away to be evacuated in the war. When I came back, she was dead."

"I know."

What more does he want?

"What was she like?" he asks.

Ruth looks at her son. He is sat up in bed, he is drinking the broth, he is enjoying it, it is doing him good. She would like to say something irritable like 'I don't know,' or 'mind your own business,' but she knows that this would be childish.

"It was such a long time ago."

"Do you have any memories?"

His bowl is empty.

"More soup?" she asks.

He shakes his head.

Yes, she has memories, of course she has memories, the issue is: does she want to remember them? She can picture her mother in her uniform leaving to go on fire watch and Ruth terrified that she would never see her again. She remembered once, before the war, going to Ruislip Lido with her mother for a picnic, the sun was shining, cheese and tomato sandwiches, white bread, watching the people in the pedal boats on the water. She remembers her mother cutting her hair in the kitchen, being told to sit still as the drifting curls tickled her nose. Why can't she tell these memories to her son?

She looks helplessly at David, who asks her: "was she a good mother?"

She remembers the argument she had had with her mother the night before she was evacuated. How Rachel, her mother, had stayed calm, had told her how much she loved her, would always love her, she wanted her to be safe, of course she didn't want to be separated from her, she said; and her, Ruth, so angry, so upset, so frightened. Rachel tried to take her in her arms and she had fought so hard until she gave in, and let her mother hold her as she wept and wept.

"Yes," she says, looking at David, "she was a good mother."

He can see that he is upsetting her. He takes her hand and closes his eyes and says:

"I'm glad."

Ruth wonders if they are good for her, these conversations with her son. Perhaps it would be better for her to leave. But she doesn't. However much she is unsettled by David, however much she is left feeling that he knows more about her than she knows herself, however much she feels that she had somehow let him down, however much the muddy swirl of memories distresses her, this is where she wants to be, where she must be, in this house, with its view and the hand-made mugs and the prints on the wall and the cold stone floor: with her son, and just her son, just David, no-one else.

Ruth stays in the background, she sees people come and go, family and friends, the nurse, the cleaner. She wants to ask them: 'what is he like, my son?' Who is he? He always seemed to her to be a sweet boy, though he was so distant from her that it was hard to be sure. And then what happened happens, and you think: what does that do to you, what did it do to him? It is a shock to realise how little you know. 'You died young,' Ruth says to herself, 'even so, it is no excuse,' she replies. 'I don't know him, did I ever know him, my own son?' She allows herself to think about Irene, for a moment, that is all, her daughter. It is too painful. She pushes the memory away.

The two grandchildren, Jess and Tom. Goodness! They are a different species. They sit by his bed for a few minutes; they tell him they love him and then go into the kitchen looking at their phones. Young people were always a puzzle to her, but now. They are like a crossword with no clues. Not even her clever son could find the answers. She would like to introduce herself to them: 'I'm Ruth. I'm David's mother. Nice to meet you. I'm your great grandmother.' Would they be interested?

Why would they care? She would like to cook them something, what do they eat, these children? They would have no idea who she is. She would mean nothing to them.

She is pleased when the son, Simon, leaves, taking the grandchildren back to London, and she is left alone with David again, and she can step out of the shadows and take her place by his bed, just like he did for her all those years ago. She lifts his head so that he can take a sip of water. She arranges his pillows, fetches an extra blanket when he is cold. She reads out the clues from the crossword for him and writes in the answers when he is able to solve them. She begins to understand the structure of the clues herself, to admire their contortions, and sometimes, with the easier ones, she comes up with the answer before he tells it to her. "Well done," he says. He seems genuinely pleased.

Later, David says to her:

"I would like you to stay with me until I die."

Ruth is upset, she doesn't want him to die, ever.

"You don't have to," he says, "if it is too much for you."

"How could I say no," she says, she means it as a joke, but there are tears in her eyes.

One day, dark and gloomy, the rain coming and going impatiently, Ruth says:

"We could do a jigsaw."

David laughs. He seems pleased, though there are no jigsaws in the house.

"We can order one online," he says.

He asks her to pass him his phone and shows her what he means. She is astonished. And so many to choose from.

"Which one do you want?" he asks her.

Ruth suggests The Hay Wain.

"Really?"

"Why not?" her turn to laugh, she is surprised at herself.

Ruth looks for a tray that will be big enough so that he can have it on his lap in bed but he says that he will just knock it over, and besides it will be good for him to get up, so she clears the desk in his office, taking her time looking at the papers and the photographs. There is a photograph of her, she looks at herself, a studio photograph, black and white, her hair was dyed then, she would have been, what, forty-eight, forty-nine, just before she became ill. How would he have come by this? She is so pleased that he has kept it, that he has it on the shelf above his desk, that he would have been able to look up sometimes and see her there.

The jigsaw arrives the next day, incredible, and she unpacks it and places the box in the middle of the desk. There is no green baize, she used to put a piece of green baize on the dining room table in the house in Stanmore, but it will be ok, they will just have to be careful. When David is awake, she helps him to get up and get into his dressing gown and he walks slowly from the living room to the office on his own and sits down on one of the chairs and catches his breath. He looks at the box.

"The Hay Wain," he says. "I always wondered: why is the wagon in the water?"

"I never noticed," Ruth says. She looks at the painting. He is right: why is the wagon in the middle of the water? Where is it going?

David takes the lid off the box and passes it to her. She fetches some scissors to open the plastic bag with all the pieces, a thousand pieces, and pours them into the box. He sifts through them and fishes out ones with a straight edge and passes them to her. She sorts them into groups, blue sky, cloud, grey cloud, white cloud, grass and trees, the stream in the bottom right corner, the roof of the building middle left. He adds pieces to her little piles and soon she is able to slot some together and the perimeter of the picture starts to take shape. They work mostly in silence, the dying son and the dead mother, side by side. They have no more questions for each other. He might say: 'there you are,' or 'this might go there,' and she says: 'thank you,' or 'no, there, I think.' Ruth fits together the dog at the bottom, three pieces. She remembers their dog, the boxer, what a good friend he had been to her.

David is not able to help her to finish the jigsaw. They had completed the edging and the black cloud at the top, and the cottage on the left, and the wagon in the water, its wheels no doubt stirring up mud on the bed of the pond, the dog barking at the back of the carter, who has turned away and is looking at the view, of fields and trees, are they sheep in the distance or hayricks? Ruth continues to work on it on her own whilst her son sleeps.

The medication holds David safe from pain now and he drifts in and out of consciousness.

One day, a nice day, with the sun filling the room with light, he sits upright and looks at his mother.

"I'm sorry," he says.

"What for?"

He searches for the words. How to say this? After all this, what *is* he sorry for?

"For putting the phone down," he says. "For coming between you and Charlie. For making life difficult for you."

Ruth takes his hand in hers. It is true, he came between her and Charlie, don't all children do this, poke their way into the spaces between their parents? But she always knew: Charlie was Charlie. When she read David's book, the book he had written just for her, she had thought: he is making this up, how does he know this, is this true, is this what I remember? She thinks now:

I loved Charlie, I did, truly, but Charlie was Charlie, and no-one was to blame for that.

"You did nothing wrong," she says to her son, placing the palm of her hand against his cheek.

He lies back on his pillow and closes his eyes. She can hear the rasping of his shallow breath.

He died in his sleep. Ruth had dozed off by his bedside and when she woke, he was gone. She stays with his body for a while, holding his hand, her son, and then she too is gone.

PART IV

INHERITANCE

IRENE

It turns out that her great aunt Irene lives in Chiswick too, a twenty-minute walk from their house. Jess asks her mum if she will come with her — 'Oh! Yes! Are you sure?' (Kate had no intention of letting her go on her own) — and they walk down to the High Street thinking they would buy flowers or pastries. Outside the greengrocers, Kate suggests a bag of figs, plump and purple, but nothing feels right, who knows what Irene might appreciate, why risk her disapproval? This is not the kind of occasion to come bearing gifts. Jess is not sure what kind of occasion it is, but they decide that, this time, nothing might be best and they don't want to be late.

They find the street, plane trees growing through the pavements shielding compact terraced houses built of brick. Very quiet. No traffic. They find Irene's house, hiding behind the screen of a leafy forsythia that has been left unchecked for too long. A short path to the front door, dark blue, recycling bins stacked unevenly to one side, no bell. Jess uses the knocker, not sure how loud she might need to knock. They wait long enough to wonder if this might be the wrong house or the wrong time, but then there are footsteps and the door is pulled open and there is Irene, short, compact, composed. Jess has worked out that Irene will be seventy-three, maybe seventy-four years old. She seems older, with grey hair and tired eyes, and also younger, with a firm presence and a strong voice. Jess is too nervous to say anything.

"Well," Irene says. "You must be Jess." There is no welcoming smile.

"I am."

"Yes," says Irene.

"And this is my mum. I hope that's all right?"

She hadn't thought until that moment that it might not be.

"Kate," says Kate.

Irene remembers to let them in, opening the door wide and leading them down a dark hallway.

"Close the door behind you, would you."

The two downstairs living rooms have been knocked through but still the space seems small and crowded. There are bookcases along one wall, overflowing; a desk in one corner, a table in another, and chairs covered with more books and magazines. There are display cabinets filled with an array of artefacts collected over a lifetime: figurines and ceramics and glassware and fragments of stone. Irene's house is an unruly museum; she is surrounded by her whole existence. She sits on the ageing sofa as if she is one of the exhibits, a part of her collection.

Kate and Jess sit on thin-legged chairs that could break under them at any moment; they haven't been sat on for a while, they might have forgotten that they are chairs. Jess perches, making herself as light as possible. Old rugs, faded and frayed, overlap at her feet. She has never been in a room like this before, she can't imagine how a room like this could come to exist, how someone could gather so many beautiful things from so many different places, how someone can manage to live a normal life in a house as refined as this.

Irene asks Jess: "would you like a cup of tea?"

Jess doesn't like tea, but here, in this room, with this woman, her great aunt, so sophisticated, she thinks it is exactly what she ought to like.

"Yes please," she says.

Irene makes her way to the kitchen. Kate stands up and finds a path to the back part of the room.

"*Mum*," says Jess anxiously.

"I'll be careful."

"Even so."

Jess stays perched on her chair.

Irene comes back, carrying a tray with some difficulty.

Kate stands: "let me." Irene is relieved to pass the tray to her.

"Jess, can you clear a space on the table?" asks Kate.

There is a low table in front of Jess that is piled with magazines and notebooks and sheets of paper. She gathers them up but is not sure where to put them.

"Over there," says Irene, pointing to the desk. "It doesn't matter."

Kate puts the tray down on the table. There is a teapot with three cups and saucers and a small jug of milk, all from a china tea set, delicately patterned.

"No biscuits," says Irene.

She speaks with a clear voice, deep and dry.

"Shall I pour?" suggests Kate.

"Yes." And then, "if you would."

As she passes Irene her cup, Kate asks "Is that a Bridget Riley?"

She had found a print in a plain white wooden frame leaning casually against a bookcase, intersecting curves of colour, amber, blue and green.

"Yes, it is. Do you like her?"

"Very much."

"I have nowhere to put it," says Irene ruefully, glancing at the walls, which are filled with a mix of pictures and hangings, masks and carvings. There has been no attempt to impose order on them. For Kate, it is like being entirely inside someone else's mind. Memories have been crammed into an insufficient space, uncurated, waiting to be recollected. The Riley print, so modern, so abstract, should be out of place amongst all these older memories, but, even on the floor, leaning, half-forgotten against a bookcase, it seems content.

"So," says Irene sharply, her cup and saucer in her hands, "you are Jess? You are my great-niece?"

"I am. I am your brother's son's daughter."

"Yes. David," says Irene.

"David was my grandfather," Jess wants to make this clear.

"Your grandfather," repeats Irene, it is so long since she has seen her brother, it is amazing for her to think of him as a grandfather.

"Yes."

"And you went to the trouble of tracking me down." Irene has a way of speaking, somewhere between a statement and a question. It is confusing.

"I hope you don't mind?" asks Jess, perched anxiously on her chair.

"I don't know," says Irene, as if she hasn't yet considered how she feels about Jess sitting there in her front room. "I don't know."

Jess is not sure what to say. She looks at Kate for help, but Kate just looks back at her; she too is unsure how best to communicate with Irene.

"This is my mother, Kate," Jess says, to fill the silence.

"You have already told me that."

"Yes. Sorry."

Irene is studying Jess, a cool appraisal of this young girl, who has taken the trouble to unearth her, to flush her out, considerable trouble she would have thought.

"Why did you want to meet me?" she asks.

There is a question, and Jess isn't entirely sure how to answer it. Instead, she says - she decides to say - she decides that this might be the time - she says:

"Can I show you something?"

She fetches from her bag the piece of paper with the family tree that she had started with her dad in the summer. Kate helps by clearing away the tea things and taking the tray back to the kitchen. Jess spreads the paper on the table, so that Irene can see it.

Irene stares at the family tree. Without her glasses, she is able to make out the names on the piece of paper, but not much else.

"There are no dates," she says.

"No," says Jess, "I thought dates are not that important."

"Absolutely," says Irene, "they are not. Not when you get to my age."

She gives off a dry laugh, a bark.

"What have you written there?" Irene is squinting at the notes that Jess has written under the names on the tree.

"What I'm interested in is what kind of people they are. Or were."

"I see."

Irene leans forward to try to read what is on the paper.

"You will need to get me my glasses, but I don't know where they are."

Jess starts to get up.

"Never mind," says Irene.

Jess sits down again. Irene points at a name on the piece of paper.

"You are at the bottom of this cascade of people," she says.

"Yes."

Irene looks up at her, narrows her eyes.

"And you want to know what has come cascading down to you."

"Yes." Jess almost shouts, she is so pleased that this elderly woman, more than anybody else, understands what she is trying to do.

Irene looks at Jess and, for the first time, smiles at her.

"And I am the missing piece," Irene says, with some satisfaction.

Jess smiles at Irene, so sharp, so quick.

"Not anymore," she says.

Jess and Irene wait in silence for Kate to come back from the kitchen. Perhaps they are both thinking: what is it that might be worth inheriting from this tumble of connections, sundered by tragedy, by folly, by wilfulness? Perhaps they are both thinking: what are the traits that Jess might want to recognise in herself?

"Is David dead?" Irene asks suddenly.

"Yes," says Jess. "He died in May."

"Was he still living in the north?"

"Yes. Lancashire," says Kate, sitting back down on her chair.

"What took him there?"

"I asked him once," this is Kate again. "He said he had to get away."

"Yes," Irene says, "that was true for us both. Sadly."

Jess wonders what she means, what it was that drove brother and sister such long ways away from their home.

"I would have gone to the funeral," Irene says. "I would

have liked to have been there. I had nothing against David. But it would have been too far for me."

"I'm so sorry," Kate is appalled. "We should have done more. We could have brought you. We didn't know about you until afterwards."

Irene waves away her apology.

"Why did you not stay in touch?" asks Jess, "you and David?"

"Oh. Now ..." says Irene.

"You don't have to ..." starts Kate, but Irene leans forward to peer at the family tree.

"Is that Charlie?" she asks Jess, pointing at a name.

"Yes, that's Charlie," says Jess, "next to Ruth. You are there, just below, next to David."

"Charlie," Irene says, and turns in on herself for a moment.

"Charlie was my father. He was ..." she hesitates, searching for the right word, "... he was a difficult man. Very difficult."

Jess looks at her, waiting for more.

"You would call him a bully now, I think, your generation. He was an angry man, very angry, very controlling. He would not let me go to university. 'Waste of time and money.' He meant women, not just me, all women. 'Waste of time'."

Jess stares at her.

"What did you do?" asks Kate.

"We argued. Terrible arguments. My father did not like to be challenged," she says drily. "In the end, I left. Never went back. I phoned once, when my mother became ill, he heard my voice, he put the phone down on me. I never saw any of them again."

There is a silence. Just as Irene does not ask questions, she does not invite them.

"Where did you go?" asks Jess finally.

"I got a job as a nanny. In Brussels. I was good at languages. I got a job at the Embassy."

Jess is awestruck.

Irene smiles at her great niece. "I was a translator, that's all. At first. I worked my way up. The Foreign Office. My whole life. I travelled the world."

Irene waves her hand at the room and its artefacts, as if to say here is the proof, if you need any. Then she says:

"I phoned him," her head lowered, her voice altered.

Jess looks at Kate, who shakes her head.

"Charlie?" asks Kate.

"When did you phone him?" asks Jess.

"Just before he died."

"That was thirteen years ago," checks Kate.

"Really?" Irene is astonished.

She looks at Kate and Jess, she is not sure why she has told them, she hadn't thought about it for such a long time, but this girl and her family tree and Charlie there in his rightful place and this girl is his blood, is my blood, and she has sought me out and she is asking me, she wants to know, she has a right to know.

Irene says firmly: "I thought he shouldn't be allowed to get away with it. He was a selfish, brutish man. He would have been eighty-four years old. I told him he was to blame. I wanted him to know, before he died, just how much damage he had done."

Jess is watching Irene's face, which is being pulled at by memories and emotions.

It is very hard to understand this woman, but Jess thinks that it will become clearer if she just waits. Kate too is looking at Irene, her story is as cluttered as her house, full of possible meanings. Irene disappears inside herself for a moment and then re-emerges, having reached a consensus with whoever else is in there, it feels like there could be a few people on that committee.

"I told him his misogyny was to blame for me leaving. I told him his pride was to blame for David leaving. I told him that his cruelty broke my mother's heart. I told him that that was why she died. I told him that he as good as killed her. I told him that his anger, his fury, his rage had damaged me and damaged David. I told him that he was like a bomb that had exploded and blown us all apart, apart from each other. He shouted at me, of course. He screamed at me. He was good at screaming. I stayed very calm. In the end, I put the phone down on him."

"Wow," says Jess. She looks down at the family tree and all the secrets it contains, its hidden history, the trail of damage. Where does it begin, she wonders, where does it end?

As if she is reading Jess' mind, Irene says:

"No children."

Jess looks up at her.

"I have no children," says Irene again. "No husband. No children."

Jess is not sure what Irene is trying to tell her.

"Did you want children?" she asks.

"Jess," says Kate, "you can't ..."

... but Irene answers: "I might have once. My father thought that that was all women were good for, having children. I chose to prove him wrong." She is defiant. "I thought it should end with me."

Jess realises that there are no photographs in this room. There is a tiled fireplace, the tiles are beautiful, green with yellow flowers. The mantlepiece, where you might expect to see photos of loved ones, has an old clock that ticks loudly, surrounded by wooden carvings, dark wood, human figures, deities, animals. There are no photographs on the table or on the desk. Maybe in her bedroom, on her bedside table. If not family, maybe friends, places. Maybe not. Jess thinks that Irene has surrounded herself with memories of her adult life and that she wants them to blot out any memories of her childhood. It seems that she does not want to give them any encouragement. And here am I, with my family tree, bringing these memories out from the buried depths into this cluttered room, into the fading light of a late afternoon in Chiswick in October.

"Did you never think to contact David when you came back to England?" Kate asks.

"When I left, I turned my back on all of them. I was so angry. I started my life again. I drifted away on the tide. When I came back, I thought ..." Irene starts, stops and then: "David and I were never close. I had been abroad for so long. We never wrote. I thought the distance was too great. The distance between us, I mean. I thought it would be too difficult. I thought it might upset him. It slipped away, things do, don't they? They slip away until they become impossible."

"Did you not see him at your father's funeral?" Kate asks.

Irene looks at her.

"I did not go to my father's funeral."

Suddenly, for the first time, Irene looks tired, sad. The effort of her life, of living her life, of fulfilling her destiny; this must be true for everyone, there comes a point when you are exhausted. Sensing this, Jess says brightly:

"I have brought something for you."

From her bag, she pulls out a copy of her grandfather David's album, '*Focus!*', and brings it over to her great aunt, his sister.

"I'll need my glasses," Irene says commandingly.

"I found them," said Kate, passing Irene her glasses. "They were in the kitchen."

Irene puts them on and takes the book from Jess and lays it on her lap.

"It's big," she says, disapprovingly.

She looks at the cover.

"This is David." She examines the photograph and reads below it:

"David Phillips. He used to have such lovely, dark curly hair. Pity."

She turns the pages, holds the book close, looks at each photograph in turn, reads David's words for each day.

"This is where he lived," she says.

"Yes," says Jess.

"It is beautiful," Irene says.

"He was very ill," says Kate, "when he did this." Then she says:

"I was very fond of David."

Irene keeps turning the pages until she comes to the photograph of Ruth.

"He had this photograph?" she asks.

"On his desk," says Kate.

"My mother," Irene says, that is all.

She comes to the photograph of Hannah.

"This is David's wife?"

"My dad added the photographs of the people," Jess says, "after grandpa David died, to keep him company somehow, I think."

"That was kind of him," says Irene.

She comes to the photographs of Howard.

"Is this your father?" she asks.

"My uncle," says Jess. "Howard."

"He died," said Kate, "very sadly."

Irene comes to the photograph on the last page. She looks hard at the picture of herself as a young woman, her smile, her hair blowing in the wind. She remembers this photograph in the dining room in Stanmore, enlarged, framed. She takes a moment to marvel at the gulf between then and now, filled by a future and a past, an imagined future and a remembered past, comparing notes.

"I look happy," she says, surprised. "I was happy."

How quickly things turned, she thinks, as if all that had gone before counted for nothing. One minute you are the star in his firmament, the next you are cast out forever. Madness. She shakes her head.

She looks again at the last two pages of the album.

"What fools we have been," she reads quietly, and then, abruptly, she laughs with pleasure.

"What?" asks Jess.

"*My* grandfather used to say that," she says. "What fools we have been."

Jess looks at the family tree to make sure who she means.

"Morris?" she asks.

"Morris. He would talk about the state of the world, which was never good, and he would always finish by saying: 'what fools we have been'."

Irene closes her eyes and they think that she might have fallen asleep. Her breathing thickens and they are not sure what to do, but then she sits up and they can see that there are tears in the corners of her eyes.

"It is time for you to go now," she says.

Jess and Kate get up quickly, apologetically.

"Before you go," Irene says to Jess, and she crosses to one of the display cabinets and opens the glass door and reaches inside for a figurine. She gives it to Jess.

"I want you to have this," she says and pushes it into her hands. "I found it when I lived in Jerusalem. It is very old."

It is a figurine of a woman. Her face has been mostly worn away. There is a long skirt that hides her feet and her arms are folded tightly under her full breasts.

"She has healing powers," says Irene, "this is one theory, it is what I prefer to believe: that people prayed to her to heal their loved ones. It is Jewish. Terra cotta. You should have it."

Jess starts to object but Irene hushes her.

"This is one small part of your inheritance, my dear," she says.

They walk down the dark corridor to the front door and out into the cool of the evening. When they reach the gate and crouch their way under the forsythia, Irene, standing in the doorway, calls out:

"Jess."

Jess turns and walks back towards the house and stops in front of her great aunt. The woman looks at the girl, admires her, admires the life ahead of her, and places the palm of her hand against Jess' cheek. Jess likes the feel of the dry skin against her face, and, looking into Irene's eyes, wonders what her great aunt is about to say to her.

The End

ACKNOWLEDGMENTS

Thanks to Gill Davis for seeing the potential in the short story that was the beginning of What Fools We Have Been; and to Pam Bain, Morgan Tanton and Peter Batty for their support, encouragement and invaluable feedback as it emerged.

Thanks to Christopher Cooke for introducing me to Denise Johnstone-Burt. Thanks to Denise for telling me to write this book and for introducing me to Laura Palmer. Thanks to Laura for her excellent input as editor and agent.

Thanks to Jamie Keegan for the artwork and to Stuart Leasor from Chiselbury Press for publishing What Fools We Have Been.

ALSO BY HANK WILLIAMS

Active Tutorial Work: A Trainer's Guide

The Essence of Managing People

The Essence of Managing Groups and Teams